T0114838

Hoot Owl Hollow

JEFF JENSWOLD

authorHOUSE®

AuthorHouse™
1663 Liberty Drive
Bloomington, IN 47403
www.authorhouse.com
Phone: 833-262-8899

Published by AuthorHouse 02/23/2021

ISBN: 978-1-6655-1780-5 (sc)
ISBN: 978-1-6655-1779-9 (e)

Library of Congress Control Number: 2021903675

Introduction

Thirteen-year-old Jay West is happy living in the city and doing as much of nothing as he can. His young life consists mostly of riding his bike, reading comic books, hanging out with his friends and occasionally working a part time job as a paper route substitute, what he hates. His mother, who is not impressed with Jay's lifestyle, arranges for him to spend a summer with his two elderly great uncles "up north." Resistant at first, Jay begrudgingly agrees to try it and see what it would be like. His Uncles' place, named Hoot Owl Hollow, is located on Lake Muckawini and near the small town of Wakanda, Wisconsin. Initially very skeptical and unimpressed with some of the primitive facilities, Jay quickly meets a number of interesting characters, makes new friends and experiences a number of new and unique experiences in the great outdoors. Young Jay ends up spending two summers at Hoot Owl Hollow, having some fun and learning about nature, fishing and a little bit about life itself.

Contents

III

SUMMER 1964

I

Summer 1963

1

Hoot Owl Hollow

The Deal

At first, Jay West didn't want any part of his mother's 'deal.' He would rather spend the summer riding his bike and just hanging with his friends in his hometown of Mendota, Wisconsin. He looked forward to his three months of freedom from school. He had just finished 8th Grade and had nothing to worry about for the quickly approaching twelve weeks-except for 'The Job.'

'The Job' was a summer newspaper route that he hated. Up every morning-way too early, picking up the huge bundle of papers, loading them on his bike (filling the big double paperboy baskets across his back tire) and pedaling his load all over the big neighborhood that made up his delivery area. The two-hour route tired him out and tried to wreck his whole day. Well, maybe most of it. Sure, he had the rest of the day free, but his parents always had "chores" and "projects" for him around the house. His free days and evenings always seemed to be overshadowed by 'The Job', waiting for him early the next morning.

Jay didn't mind actually delivering the newspapers all that much. He liked riding his bike and liked being outdoors, especially in the early mornings when the sun was just coming up and he had the neighborhood to himself. That part was ok, unless it was raining; then it was awful. What he did mind was the pickiness of his customers. They complained if the paper was late; they complained if the paper was early; they complained if it wasn't exactly where they wanted it left (between the doors or in the

1

mailbox or on the front porch). And he especially hated it when it came time to 'collect.' Part of 'The Job' included face to face visits with his customers, usually once a month, to get them to pay for their subscriptions.

Most of his customers were nice. Some were not; some made you think they were parting with their last few dollars (these were often the same customers with a Cadillac or a Lincoln or two in their driveway).

Jay dreaded the thought of delivering newspapers all summer. There were so many better, more fun things to do. "I want to quit!"

His constant complaining was wearing on his parents' patience. "You need to do something," his mother told him. "You can't spend all day just 'hanging out' or whatever it is that you do. Besides, your job gives you some spending money."

Jay still complained until his mother finally had enough. "I've had enough," she announced. "I've got an idea and a deal for you! Your father and I have been talking to your Grandpa Gary and we came up with something that should make you happy, give you some fun things to do and even make a little spending money." Jay was skeptical, especially because of his mother mentioning the word "deal." Her past "deals" for him usually involved work.

His mother pressed on, "Here's the idea. You know Grandpa's two brothers, Clarence and Robert. They live up north, near Wakanda. They're retired and both are widowers and moved in together to save money. They have a good size place on Lake Muckawini. They're getting up there in age and its all they can do to keep up the maintenance and repair around their place. Anyway, Grandpa and I talked to them and they agreed that they'd like to have you spend the summer with them. You'll like it. It'll be fun."

"What?" Jay asked in surprise. "No way! I have friends here and I have lots of things I want to be doing with them! I wouldn't know anyone up there!"

"You know Uncle Clarence and Uncle Robert and you can meet other people. They know a lot of people."

Jay remembered that both of his great-uncles liked to fish and do outdoors-y things. They seemed nice enough. "I guess they're ok but I haven't seen them all that much; maybe a couple of times a year. Plus, they're old."

"Now here's the deal. You can quit the paper route if you go," his mother said. That got Jay's attention, but just a little.

"Look, you like being outside, you like to fish, you like wandering around the woods. You could help them around the place from time to time and they'd pay you for your work. You could work as much or as little as you want."

"What kind of work?"

"According to Grandpa, maybe some painting, some lawn work, cutting wood, helping them fix things, that kind of stuff. Plus, they have a new garden tractor I bet they'd let you drive."

Jay was getting a little more interested, but … "all summer?"

"It'll only be for a little less than three months, most of June, July and August and then it'll be back to school in September."

"All summer?" Jay asked again. "And no more paper route?"

"Yes," his mother replied. "We could maybe come up and visit once in a while and maybe Grandpa and Grandma too, but since they live in Illinois..."

"Can I have friends visit?"

"We'll see. But Grandpa says there are some kids your age nearby and maybe you could make some new friends."

"Sounds like prison," Jay said.

"It's not, and," she reminded him, "they do a lot of fishing and lots of nature things; things you like to do too."

"Yeah," Jay had to admit. Maybe this deal wouldn't be so bad after all. He could give it a try and if things went really bad, his parents would have to let him come home (wouldn't they?). And he could still be done with The Job; hopefully once and for all.

"Ok." He nodded. "Deal. I'll give it a try."

The Arrival

After 4 hours in the car with his parents, Jay was more than happy to get out. His dad had old people music on the radio and refused to change it. His mother read some, which was good but then she wanted to play games, which was bad.

"Let's count cars; you count red ones and I'll count blues ones" or "you count cows on your side and I'll count them on mine" or "let's see how many makes of cars we can count."

The trip seemed to take forever but they eventually pulled off of a paved road onto a long, narrow gravel driveway. They ended up in a yard with a log house, a big shed and several smaller buildings. A greenish-blue lake sparkled behind some trees.

"Here we are, Jay. Hoot Owl Hollow!" His dad exclaimed.

Two elderly men were standing on the cabin's porch. Clarence and Robert walked over to greet them. Clarence was tall and lean and was a little older than his brother. He had short, grey hair and a cigarette hanging out his mouth. Robert was shorter, stockier and mostly bald. His glasses made his eyes look large.

"They don't look like brothers," Jay muttered to his mother.

"Clarence and your grandpa take after your great grandfather and Robert takes after your great grandmother."

"Haven't seen you folks in a long while," Clarence said. Hugs and handshakes all around. "Jay seems like he's still growing." He stuck his hand out to Jay. "You remember that they call me C.C.? And he's The Big Bobber?"

Jay nodded.

"Welcome to our stately manor on the lake."

"Named Hoot Owl Hollow?" Jay asked.

"Yep. Lots of owls around here. Wait 'til you start hearing them at night. Can make the hair on your neck stand straight up if you ain't used to them."

Great, Jay thought to himself.

"But we've got a lot of other critters," Clarence joined in. "We have chipmunks, squirrels, raccoons, deer, geese, tons of different kinds of birds and lots of other things; even a bear or two that may wander through in the spring."

"Isn't spring over and the bears moved on?" Jay asked.

"Almost, but not quite."

Great, Jay thought to himself.

Hoot Owl Hollow was organized in a cluttered way: a bright red 1961 International pickup truck sat by a shed. A big blue and white 1957 Buick was parked in front of the cabin. An older, rusty pickup truck, a 1939 International, sat far back in the woods. It was covered with leaves and vines and didn't look like it had been driven in a long time.

There were bird houses and feeders everywhere; a garden was just getting started at the edge of the woods. A small red Wheel Horse garden tractor could be seen through an open door of one of the small sheds.

"What's that?" Jay asked, pointing to another small, odd looking building.

"That's our deluxe bathroom."

"Weird." Jay figured they were joking with him. He didn't notice the glances and smiles that passed between his parents.

A path led to the lake; a rickety pier extended about 30 feet into the water. An aluminum fishing boat with an outboard motor was tied up to it and a 12-foot wooden boat was secured to the other side of the pier. A decent looking boathouse sat at the edge of the water.

C.C. waved his hand towards the lake. "That's Lake Muckawini. The fishing is pretty good; lots of different fish and other things in there. We don't have too much big boat traffic or heavy fishing pressure, except on weekends in the summer."

"Lake Muckawini, that's a weird name," Jay said. "Why's it named that?"

"They say that the Indians who first settled around here named it that. I think it means 'mischievous child' in their language."

"In other words, spoiled brat in our language," The Big Bobber added.

The lake was a pretty blueish-green and fairly good sized. There were also several other lakes of various sizes close by. A lot of Summer cottages and some year-round homes sat around the lakes. Many of the properties had been given names: White Pine, Oak Lane, Belleview, Parkland, Tall Pines, Easylivin, Back Ache Acres, and of course, Hoot Owl Hollow. Many of the names were prominently displayed on signs, some fancy, some not, at the end of each driveway.

There were about a couple of dozen other places on Lake Muckawini; some year around houses and some vacation cottages.

"Over there," C.C. pointed to a larger white house, "is a neighbor of ours we call 'Fisherman Andy'. You'll be meeting him."

"And two doors past him is Miss Norma," The Big Bobber chimed in.

"You should know," C.C. muttered.

The Big Bobber shot him a glance, "She's a friend and there's nothing more going on between us."

"So you say." C.C. then looked back to Jay. "There're only a few rules. Let us know where you're going and when you'll be back. You can take the boat out when you want but you gotta check with one of us first. We'll supply you with fishing gear and bait, but you have to clean and share any 'keeper' fish you bring back. Use the big AM radio on the porch when you want but keep the volume low, especially at night and especially if you're listening to that rock and roll."

"I dunno about that," said The Big Bobber. "Some rock and roll is ok."

C.C. frowned at him and continued his welcome speech. "We go to town once a week and go to the dump every two weeks. If we do anything socially with the neighbors, you can come along if you want, or not, as long as we say its ok."

"Can I drive the truck?" Jay asked.

"Maybe when you get older."

"The little tractor?"

"We'll see. Which brings us to chores and working for an allowance."

"Allowance?" asked Jay.

"Naw, not really; we'll pay you 50 cents an hour for any work you do that aren't daily chores. We usually do any work around here in the morning, eat lunch and then fish or nap in the afternoon."

"But not always," The Big Bobber added. "Sometimes we mix it up. But we always leave time for fishing."

"Any other kids around here?" Jay asked.

"A few. You'll meet them soon enough. And not too many trouble makers around, thanks to Big John."

"Big John?" Jay asked. "Who's he?"

"He's the Muckawini Township Constable. Big guy. Doesn't take much crap from anyone, but if you watch yourself, you won't have a problem with him."

"Then there's Norma; she's got a couple of cute granddaughters," this from The Big Bobber.

"Yeah," said C.C, "and they're around quite a bit. Plus there are some other kids you 'll meet soon enough. Like Abbie's grandsons Harvey and Willie. They come to stay by her a lot in the summer."

"We're having a little party next weekend; it'll be The Big Bobber's birthday on Saturday and a bunch of the neighbors and some other folks will be comin' over. You'll get your chance to meet a bunch of them then." He grabbed two of Jay's bags and headed into the house. "Come on, we'll get you settled in."

Jay and his parents followed him in. The Big Bobber headed for the shed, saying he needed to feed the birds.

The house was a large, winterized semi-restored log cabin. It was only one story and had no basement but it was nicely furnished. In spite of its age and lack of a few luxuries, it was comfortable in both Summer and Winter. The brothers had purchased the house and its 20-acre wooded lot years before, when they were both still working and their wives were alive. They had used it as a summer cottage during that time and had entertained many friends and family members over those years. Following their respective retirements and the loss of each of their wives, they decided to remodel the house, move in together and live there full time.

A large wood stove and a fireplace backed up by a large propane heater provided adequate heat if and when needed. In very cold weather, large piles of stacked firewood added additional heat. The propane tanks were serviced by the owner of the hardware store in Wakanda, the closest town. Electric power lines from the road provided power to their lights, stove, refrigerator, several radios and a medium size black and white television set. The TV could bring in four somewhat local channels (unless it was very windy, raining or snowing hard.) The radios could usually pick up an adequate number of stations; even some distant ones on clear nights.

A private well provided cold water to the kitchen. There was no water heater so water had to be heated in pots on the stove. Baths were taken in the lake in the summer. Winter made baths a little trickier. The brothers hadn't been kidding; there was no inside bathroom. The toilet facilities consisted of the outhouse that Jay had just seen outside. "Next year, we're planning on having a septic system put in and adding an inside bathroom and water heater," The Big Bobber said.

In addition to the kitchen and a living room, there were four bedrooms and a large enclosed porch that provided a nice view of the lake.

"C.C" was short for Clarence's nickname, 'cane pole' which was due to his preference for using his cane pole for all kinds of fishing; bass, panfish, trout. He claimed to have caught some northerns on his cane pole but since no one could remember ever seeing him do that, this claim was doubted by some.

C.C. was an army veteran, having served and had seen action in both World War I and World War II. He retired after the end of WWI with the rank of Lt. Colonel. He then had a farm for a number of years before selling it and retiring once again in 1960. He now received a veterans' pension as well as a Social Security check each month. Although he had adequate money, he would sometimes supplement it by working at local odd jobs around the area for cash.

The Big Bobber's nickname came partially from his use of very large bobbers over sucker minnows for fishing northerns and muskies. Unlike C.C., when The Big Bobber spoke of the large fish he had caught, he was believed by all. The Big Bobber was also a big fan of rockabilly music: Carl Perkins, Johnny Cash, Elvis, Jerry Lee Lewis and his favorite singer: The Big Bopper. So, of course, he became known as The Big Bobber. He had retired several years earlier after many years of working as an engineer for the Chicago and Northwestern Railroad in Milwaukee. Like C.C., he now had adequate retirement income, between his railroad pension and Social Security. The Big Bobber now spent much of his time fishing, checking things out in the woods and working on some project or another. Both of the old guys were widowers. C.C.'s wife had passed away from an illness five years earlier. The Big Bobber's had died in an accident a few years before that. Neither had remarried (at least not yet) and neither of them had any children. They now shared expenses and shared many interests so it worked out pretty well. They had their spats but got along with each other most of the time.

Jay was assigned to his own bedroom; a small 10x12 room paneled in knotty pine. It was between C.C.'s and The Big Bobber's bedrooms. "You can set it up as you want but don't overdo it," Jay was told. "No girly posters and pick up your own trash and keep it sort of picked up. There may be times, depending on who shows up to spend the night, when you 'll have to sleep a night or so on a couch on the porch."

Jay didn't even spend his first night in his newly assigned bedroom. His parents took it over and he got a couch on the porch. He had trouble falling asleep; the owls kept hooting.

Later the next morning, after a hearty breakfast (Jay's mother had insisted on cooking 'for the men'), his parents took him aside as they got ready to head home. "So, what do you think so far?" his mother asked.

All in all, Jay thought the place all looked kind of cool but he still wasn't sure if he would like spending his whole summer vacation there. "I don't know about being here all summer and not knowing anyone," he said.

"You'll meet people; there are other kids around and should be a lot of interesting things to do."

Jay shrugged. "I guess it'll be ok." He waved goodbye as his parents got into their car and pulled out of the driveway.

2

The Big Bobber's Big Birthday Bash

Jay had been at Hoot Owl Hollow for one week. It was now Saturday and the brothers were up extra early. C.C. was out in the yard and The Big Bobber was banging around in the kitchen. Jay woke up and thought that there was a lot of activity for 8 in the morning. He wandered into the kitchen, sat down at the kitchen table, rubbed his eyes and asked, "What's going on?"

"We're having a party," The Big Bobber said. "This afternoon. Gotta bunch of people coming over."

"Here? What for?"

"Well, it's my birthday today, plus the party is also kind of a welcome party for you. It'll be your chance to meet some of the neighbors and others; some folks will be bringing their kids or grandkids. Hot dogs, burgers and corn on the cob on the grill and folks are bringing other food."

"Oh, yeah. It's your birthday today. Happy Birthday." Jay remembered. "What's for breakfast?"

The Big Bobber tossed him a box of corn flakes. "Milk is where it usually is."

C.C. came in as Jay was munching on soggy cornflakes. "Got the two picnic tables set up. One has a broken leg so I propped it up with a concrete block. Brought out some lawn chairs too; should be enough places for everyone to sit. Next, I gotta get the old grill out and clean it up." He poured himself a cup of coffee, sat down and lit up a cigarette.

"So who's all coming?" Jay asked.

"A few neighbors and some others. You don't know any of them yet but you soon will."

The Big Bobber pulled a note with scribbling on it off the countertop. "Let's see." He peered at the list. "Uncle Tom. He's an older guy, not really anybody's uncle. We just call him that. Known him forever. He comes up from Rock Falls to stay about every other week. Likes to fish but is a little set in his ways, especially about fishing."

"He means well," C.C. pointed out. "And he does know something about fishing. Really loves it."

"That he does. A good guy. We're probably the closest thing he has to family. He's a widower. Has two kids with their own families but they're all in California. He likes to come around here and we don't mind having him."

"Fisherman Andy is coming. He lives just down the road, also on the lake. He's a definitely a self-named fishing expert; he just doesn't know as much about it as he thinks he does. But he's ok. He likes hanging around too; he fishes a lot but doesn't stray off Lake Muckawini very much. Uncle Tom, on the other hand, likes fishing for different types of fish and likes trying other lakes."

"And rivers," added The Big Bobber.

"Speaking of fishing, then there's Fisherwoman," C.C. said.

"Fisherwoman?" asked Jay "Is that her name? Doesn't she have a real name?"

"Yeah, it's Delphine but you never want to call her that. She'll kick your butt. She goes by the name of Dee but also doesn't mind 'Fisherwoman.' She's kind of a hard case and you don't want to get on her bad side, but she can be nice if she likes you."

"And she really knows what she's doing when it comes to fishing."

"Yes she does. She lives over by Casey's Corners and has been on pretty much every body of water in this and surrounding counties."

"When you fish with her, and you will be, you want to pay attention," C.C. advised. "She always catches fish."

"Abbie, who lives down the road, is also coming. She has two granddaughters close to your age who are usually around in the summer. Maybe you'll meet them. They're nice girls but kinda shy."

"Don't forget The Warden."

"Oh yeah, Warden Jim. He's the game warden around here. He patrols the whole county but spends a lot of time in this area. He's a nice guy but a stickler for rules. He's very knowledgeable about all the backroads, fishing spots…"

"…And violators." C.C. finished the sentence. "He's a friend of ours, though. Has a lot of wild stories. Folks around here either love him or hate him."

"Norma is also coming. She has two grandsons. One is a teenager and the other is several years younger. They visit her from time to time. They seem like ok kids and will probably come with her this afternoon."

C.C. winked at Jay. "The Big Bobber is sweet on Norma; she makes him cookies and other treats all the time. She'll bring other food today too, and not just for The Big Bobber. He can share with the rest of us."

"Yeah? Let me tell you about old C.C. and Abbie!" The Big Bobber bristled. "Talk about being sweet on someone! Good old C.C. is always going over to her place to 'help' her out with all kinds of chores and projects. Things she says she can't do herself and needs a 'man to help her with.' Complicated tasks like changing a light bulb, taking out her trash, helping her in the yard. But she drives all over creation and is very active in all kinds of things."

C.C. changed the topic. "Leechman's on the list, right?"

"Yep, he's planning on coming."

"Leechman?" Jay asked.

"Yeah, his real name is Mark but we call him Leechman. He runs the best bait shop around here, but of course it's the only one. He's a pretty good fisherman himself and is especially good with a fly rod. When he isn't using a fly rod, he likes to only use leeches. Claims they're the best live bait for every kind of fish."

"He has a nice store," C.C. added. "Sells a lot of tackle and other stuff, too. He also always knows what's biting and where and when. Gets a lot of information from his customers and friends. But he also knows that fishermen often lie about the fish they caught-or didn't-and where they caught them-or didn't."

"True enough," The Big Bobber agreed. "But he pretty much knows who he can believe and he's good at separating out the bull crap from the truth."

"Leechman has a couple of kids. They're about your age, give or take a year or so. Leechman's kind of a young pup himself. Maybe 40 or so," C.C. said. "Got shared custody of them after his divorce. His 'ex' lives in Chicago; she likes the big city. Apparently doesn't like it here, doesn't like fishing or being bait shop wife. Guess that doesn't have enough social status for her. Anyway, he has his kids every other weekend so maybe they'll be here too."

People started arriving by 1:30. Jay noticed that both C.C. and The Big Bobber had cleaned up not only the yard and the house but cleaned themselves up, too. Shaved and showered and dressed in nice clothes.

The first one to arrive was Fisherman Andy, closely followed by Fisherwoman. Andy brought a 6 pack of Bullfrog beer with a bow on it. Fisherwoman brought a package of filleted crappies. Uncle Tom arrived soon after and Leechman and his two kids came next. He introduced Lester and Linda to Jay and he went over to sit with Fisherwoman; they both opened a Bullfrog beer.

"Call me Les, not Lester," the boy told Jay right away. "I hate the name Lester."

Linda nodded in agreement. "He gets mad when people call him that."

They both said they liked coming up here to visit their dad but Linda admitted that she sometimes got a little bored. "sometimes, there's not much to do around here," complained Linda. "it's not like Chicago.

"That's 'cuz you get bored easy," Les said to her. "And thank goodness it's not like Chicago."

Norma came with her grandsons. The older one's name was Harvey; the younger one, Willie. They already knew Les and Linda. Jay introduced himself; he and Harvey hit it off right away. They found they were the same age and both liked many of the same things: fishing, being outdoors and both had started listening to some of the rock and roll music the older folks did not care for.

"Believe it or not, I can get WLS on my grandma's radio, but I have to wait until she falls to sleep to listen to it," Harvey said. "Some night you should sleep over and we can listen to it. It has a strong signal at night. Can't always get it clear but a lot of the time I can.'"

"He keeps me awake," Willie complained.

"Where's WLS out of?" Jay asked.

"Chicago, a long ways away. Like where most of the old people around here came from," Harvey answered.

"Its Les and my favorite station when we are with our mom," Linda offered.

"I agree with Linda that it can sometimes get a little boring, especially if it rains, but we make our own fun," Harvey said. "And Abbie's got two granddaughters who visit her a lot, Jackie and Jody. They're about our ages and tomboyish, but cute. Jackie, the older one is really outgoing and adventurous and is a lot of fun. Jody is quieter and a little shy but she can be fun too. She's called 'Jo'. They like hanging around outside; in the woods and around the lake.

"Yeah," said Linda. "It's nice to have some other girls to hang around with."

"We're usually allowed to play outside until after dark, if our particular adult 'keepers' know where we are," Les said. "We have a couple of tree forts in the woods and we're allowed to swim and take boats out on the lake."

"Unless it's storming, then we can't," Linda added. "That I get, but there are some other rules that are just dumb."

"Like what?" Jay asked.

"Like having to wait an hour after lunch before we can go swimming. And like having to come in for lunch right at noon. They even have a bell they ring to call us to come in."

"Yeah," agreed Les. "What's that hour thing about all about, anyway? And why do we have to eat at noon if we're not hungry right then?" No one had an answer.

They sat together and ate hot dogs, hamburgers and potato chips; a couple of them tried some vile-looking barbeque on a bun. No one liked it, except Jay, who thought it was ok. "Who made this?" He asked.

"My grandma did," Harvey answered, sticking out his tongue. Willie wolfed down two of them.

"Let's go for a walk," Les suggested. He yelled over to the group of adults. "We're going to check out the woods. Be back in a little bit."

The adults smiled and waved back. "Have fun."

They headed down a trail that ran through the woods, Harvey in the lead. Shortly, he stopped and pointed. "There are our tree forts," he said to Jay, pointing at two wooden structures ahead of them. They were about 6 feet off the ground and nestled in the branches of several large oaks; about 30 feet from each other. The closest one was just a big platform with a handmade ladder going up to it. The other was a larger, box-like thing with a small door; it also had a ladder.

"Cool," Jay said.

"We built them ourselves," Les said. "With the help of Jackie and Jo," added Linda.

"The adults all thought it was cool. C.C. and The Big Bobber even donated some of the wood and lent us some tools to build them," Harvey told Jay.

The platform tree fort was big enough to hold all five of them. They sat down and Les reached into his pocket and pulled out several stubby cigarette butts.

"What's with this?" Jay asked.

"They're from our dad, but he didn't really give them to me. He usually only smokes half a cigarette at a time, butts it out and sticks it in his pocket, planning to smoke it later. He forgets about them and I find them in his shirt pocket."

"He doesn't know you have them?" Jay asked.

"Naw, he doesn't always remember he had them in there." Les lit one up and offered one to Linda who said no. Harvey took one. Willie was not offered one and was warned to keep his mouth shut about this. "I know, I know," Willie said.

The last one was offered to Jay. "I'll try it," he said. Jay took a puff and started coughing. "It's my first time."

"Don't take such a big puff," Les counseled. "Just a little." Jay tried a little puff but coughed again. "You'll get used to it," Les said.

"Maybe," Jay answered. "C.C. smokes Chesterfields and I've seen him do the same thing with his half-cigarette butts. The Big Bobber doesn't smoke cigarettes but I've seen him with a cigar every once in a while."

"Not in front of my grandma, he doesn't," Harvey laughed.

"What else do you guys do around here?" Jay asked. "Besides smoke cigarette butts?"

"Well, we play cards in the tree forts and we take hikes through the woods," Linda told him. Sometimes we split up into teams and see who can find the neatest things in the woods. Like a contest."

They headed back to where the adults were still eating and visiting. By then Abbie and her granddaughters had arrived.

The two newly arrived girls came over to meet up with their friends. The taller one went up to Jay. "I'm Jackie and this is Jo."

"Hi. I'm Jay."

"We know. Your uncles were just telling us all about you."

They all sat down in a circle on the lawn. "So, Jay, you like to fish?" Jackie asked.

"Sure."

"That's good!"

"Like to play games, do stuff outside and swim?"

"Sure."

"Good. Its good that you're here," she added, "now the teams will be even; girls against the boys."

"So, you guys are the only kids around?" Jay asked.

"Yes and no," answered Linda. "Every summer there are tourists who rent some of the cottages around the lake and some families have kids about our age. But they're only here for a week or two and then they're gone.

"But some come back every year," added Les. "So we get to see some of them more than once. Plus sometimes of the other 'lake natives' have relation that include kids and they may come around once in a while but not regularly."

"So yeah, it's basically been the five of us older ones," Harvey said.

"Six now," said Jay. "And if you count little Willie, it makes seven."

3

The Outhouse

Jay finally used the outhouse for the first time. He had been putting it off for a couple hours after arriving, but nature had stopped calling and started yelling and the time had come.

"So, this is the bathroom?" Jay asked C.C., who was raking leaves nearby. "Looks like it'll fall over any minute," he said, nervously eying the tall, little building.

"It's solid and has stood tall through many big thunderstorms and high winds over many years. Besides, it's not a bathroom. It's an outhouse, a privy, a john or even a crapper, but it ain't no 'bathroom.'"

"Looks like it has a bunch of spiders, snakes and other nasty things living in there; all of them hungry."

C.C. pulled the door open. "Well, maybe few, but they won't bite you. Look here, it's got a seat and even a couple of rolls of toilet paper. And look at these decorations on the walls!"

On the four walls were signs, some funny, some not so much-but all tacky: 'The job isn't complete until the paperwork is done' and 'We don't pee in your pool, don't swim in our toilet' and 'Always aim before you shoot' and 'I'm a little stinker (a cartoon skunk holding its nose).'

"Nice touch," was all Jay could say. "But the spiders...I'm not so worried about peeing but sitting down with a bare butt. There's gotta be millions of Black Widows, Tarantulas and other killers waiting to take a bite of my butt and kill me with poison."

"Nah," C.C. tried to reassure him. "No killer spiders around here, maybe some daddy long legs, a few wolf spiders and some other little guys here and there, but nobody dangerous, painful or poisonous."

"I still don't like it. And it stinks in here."

"Well, of course it stinks a little bit. After all, it is a crapper and it's not like you're going to be spending a lot of time in here."

"It stinks a lot. And what happens if, or more like when, the hole fills up?"

"We use lime. Put a few shovelfuls down the hole every week or two. That's what's in the big bags in the shed."

"I don't get it."

"See, the lime eats the crap. It breaks it down and makes it rot away and it doesn't build up so fast. If we didn't use the lime, we'd be digging new holes all the time and be moving the privy around a lot. This way, we can go a fair bit of time without having to dig a new hole. Plus, the lime keeps the stink tolerable."

Jay looked down the hole, keeping a wary eye out for spiders. "Ugh!"

C.C. had a thought. "That could be one your jobs while you're here. Tossing lime down the hole every week."

Jay was not enthused about that.

"Or if you'd rather, you could get down in there and shovel the crap out with the spade. But that might not be much fun."

"Ok, I'll do the lime, but I don't need to get too close or dirty, do I?"

"Nah, you could do it in your Sunday suit."

"I ain't got a Sunday suit," Jay replied.

They came outside and C.C. closed the door. "What's with the latch on the door?" Jay asked. "I get the latch on the inside, but why one on the outside?"

"Keeps the racoons and squirrels out. Don't want them going in when nobody's around. They'd steal the toilet paper and make a mess of things."

"Sounds like the boys' bathroom back at school," Jay said.

As time went by, Jay used the outhouse, but only when he absolutely had to. When nature called, he looked for a tree or bushes that would provide a little privacy. He kept an eye out for poison ivy, poison oak and poison sumac, (all of which he quickly learned to identify) and, of course, killer spiders, especially when he had #2 business. He hid a roll of toilet paper in the shed for any outdoor business he may have.

One morning, Jay accidently locked The Big Bobber in the outhouse. He bumped the outside latch as he swept June bugs off the outside of the door. Before long, he heard some banging and yelling from inside the privy. "Hey! Open the goldang door!" Mumbled cuss words followed.

"Sorry", Jay said, opening the latch and releasing the captive. "It was an accident."

A couple of weeks later, Uncle Tom showed up; his 1962 Pontiac station wagon roared up the driveway and slid to a stop at the end of the driveway, raising a cloud of dust. Uncle Tom drove a station wagon because he was always hauling a lot of fishing equipment with him everywhere he went. He always drove fast and defended the use of his heavy foot by claiming it was all right because he could stop fast too. With his rosy red cheeks, a fringe of gray hair peeking out from under his black fedora, a sizable belly and glasses that kept slipping down his nose, he looked like a clean-shaven, displaced Santa Claus. He dragged his suitcase and a large, very smelly bag out of the car.

"What'd ya bring us," The Big Bobber asked. "Supper?"

"Better than that! Got a whole mess of stink baits for catfish. Carefully aged chicken guts and assorted parts, moldy balls of bread, and a whole mess of cheese and other stuff that may smell a bit but is irresistible to the big "cats.""

"You're got that right about the 'mess' part, but don't be putting all that in the fridge in here. Take it out to the old beer and bait fridge in the shed."

Jay and Jackie were sitting on at the picnic table and playing a card game when Uncle Tom walked past them with his stinky bag. "Hey there, kids! How's my young fishing buddy, Jay? And hello to you, Miss Jaqueline!"

"Taking out the garbage?" Jackie asked, holding her nose.

"Hah! Shows what you kids know. Its topnotch bait for catfish."

"Smells like catfish already; catfish that're dead and have been rotting in the hot sun for a couple weeks."

Uncle Tom was his usual jovial self and liked teasing Jay. "Got yourself a girlfriend now-eh Jay? Miss Jacqueline seems like a nice girl."

"Nah, just friends."

"Hah! When's the wedding?"

"No wedding, just friends." Jay reddened, and Uncle Tom chuckled as he continued on his way.

A little later, he came out of the house with a few newspapers in hand, heading for the outhouse. "Gonna catch up on some reading, if you know what I mean," he chuckled as he went inside and shut the door. The inside latch clicked.

"Watch out for spiders," Jay cautioned Uncle Tom. He turned to Jackie. "Watch this." He snuck over to the closed door and quietly latched it from the outside. He snuck back to the picnic table and sat down. "Just wait."

They soon heard the click as the inside latch was opened, then a pushing on the door, then some light tapping on the door and then louder pounding and then, "Hey! Let me out! Anybody out there? Door's stuck!" Then even louder banging.

Jay and Jackie were quietly giggling. It was all they could do to keep from laughing out loud.

"Hey! Was it you kids? Bet it was! You out there? Let me out right now!"

The ruckus brought The Big Bobber over. "What's going on?" He asked, but one look told him exactly what was happening. He played along.

"I'm in here," Uncle Tom yelled.

"Well, come on out."

"I can't come out!!"

"Come on, Uncle Tom. Whatcha doing in there? Its too nice a day to spend it in the crapper! But if you insist on staying, I can bring you more paper-both kinds if you need some."

"The door's stuck; it had to be those juvenile delinquent kids locked me in! Open the door! Please?"

"You remember, Uncle Tom? In the old days? Someone would get themselves locked in the privy and then danged if somebody wouldn't tip the whole crapper over, passenger and all. Made a hell of a mess if I recall."

"You wouldn't dare do that! Come on, help me out!"

"You're right, it'd make too big a mess," The Big Bobber said. He then whispered to the kids, "get on outa here. Take a walk."

After they left and were out of sight, The Big Bobber opened the door on a sputtering, red-faced Uncle Tom.

"Well, howdy-do, Uncle Tom! And look here, the latch was just a little caught. It musta slipped closed when you slammed the door shut."

"I didn't slam it, I shut it real nice."

"Even so, looks like you musta done it to yourself, real nice."

"Bet it was those kids. They're always messing with me."

"C'mon Uncle Tom, you all mess with each other. Besides, I don't see those kids around, do you?"

Uncle Tom looked around, shook his head, clutched the crumbled newspapers and headed for the cabin. "Well, better get that latch fixed" he said, "it could happen to you, ya know."

The Big Bobber took a whiff in the now-open door. "Phew, maybe you should toss a little extra lime down that hole."

4

Wakanda

Tuesday. Town Day. The Big Bobber, C.C. and Jay climbed into The Big Bobber's big Buick Road Master, along with four baskets of dirty clothes and headed into 'town'.

'Town' was Wakanda, a small city of a couple thousand people. (The City Limits sign advertised pop. 1,900 in winter/5,000 in summer). The distance to town was only 10 miles from Hoot Owl Hollow but each Tuesday's event was treated as a major excursion.

The brothers would spend Tuesdays getting their clothes washed, buying gas, stopping by Tully's Coffee Shop, buying groceries, visiting the hardware store, eating lunch at Millie's Diner and, of course, an after lunch stop at Caroline's Billiard Hall. An unspoken purpose of these excursions was to catch up on the latest local news and gossip. The actual amount of time spent in town depended on who they would run into during their various stops.

The first stop was always the Wishy-Washy Laundromat. (25 cents washer, 10 cent dryer). The brothers' method was to lug their laundry into the building and then approach someone to wash and dry their clothes for them for $10. They were selective; their washer/dryer helper had to be female (they didn't trust men to know what to do) and look honest. They always found someone, often quickly because the laundromat was usually busy when they would show up. Today however, there was only a three-member family in the place; Ma, Pa and an obnoxiously loud teenage son. They carried the clothes baskets in and sat down to wait for help to show up.

The entertainment provided for customers while they waited consisted of old magazines (all had any coupons and other things already cut out of them), that focused to focus on recipes and housekeeping and keeping a marriage alive. Once in a while on lucky days, a dog-eared Field and Stream or Outdoor Life or a relatively recent newspaper would show up. There was also a large bulletin board with local things for sale, jobs and various services and small businesses.

Today, the obnoxious teenage boy was loudly reading a posted ad to his parents. "Look here, a free parrot! Pa, let's get us a parrot!"

"Ask your ma!"

"Ma?"

"Hell, no!"

"C'mon, Ma. I'll take care of it!"

"Ha! Just like you take care of the dogs and cats, and chickens and rabbits?"

"C'mon Ma, it can live in the house, sleep in my room."

"No way, no how!"

These two each had only one volume setting-loud. It sounded to Jay that this argument was going to last a while. Luckily, at about that time, a middle-aged woman came in with her own laundry and, after a brief negotiation, agreed to take care of the brothers' laundry for them, cash in advance. The loud family-mother and son-were still arguing about the parrot (Pa was studying a recipe for lemon pie in a magazine) as C.C. led them out of the laundromat.

"I hate going to that place," The Big Bobber said as they climbed into the car and headed to McCabe's Hardware Store.

After a quick stop at Robert's "Phillips 66" to fill up the Buick's huge gas tank with 'Ethyl' (and check the oil, the tires and wash the windows), they arrived at Shamus McCabe's store.

McCabe Hardware had three stories, packed with everything imaginable: plumbing, electrical, automotive, fishing stuff, bird seed, even some local souvenirs (most of them tacky). You could get saws, knives and axes sharpened, keys cut, and free advice on anything and everything. Mac, as he was always called, knew where every nail and screw, every pipefitting, every can of STP, every tool, every birdfeeder was in his store.

"G'mornin', Mac."

"Mornin' boys!" Mac had come directly to Wakanda from Scotland almost 50 years ago. He had run the hardware store for the past 30 years. He still had a hint of a Scottish brogue and loved to talk.

The Big Bobber produced a list of what was needed: bird seed, a new hammer, a battery powered lantern, a couple boxes of .22 long rifle shells, a pair of gloves. Jay was treated to a cheap cane pole and a three pack of cork bobbers. "And I need an extra keys made for the Buick." The Big Bobber was always losing his car keys.

They visited with Mac for a while, catching up on local news: One of the two local theaters was closing, a new Standard gas station was opening, an obscure county western band was going to play in the bandstand on the town square on Friday night.

"And bad news, boys. Gas is going up to 30 cents a gallon soon! But some good news-8 pack bottles of Bull Frog beer are on sale at the Trading Post for 89cents."

After loading their purchases into the Buick, they headed to Tully's Coffee Shop for some coffee and local gossip. A half dozen locals were talking over coffee cups and fresh donuts. Greetings were exchanged. They found seats and ordered coffee; Jay got a grape Nehi. Important local matters were being discussed.

"Mary Jane's daughter got pregnant and she was sent to Duluth to stay with an aunt."

"Ike and Helen visited Clay and Agnes last Tuesday but left early when Clay accused Ike of cheating at Gin Rummy."

"You all know those old sisters, Ginny and Doris; well, they don't talk to each other and yet they've been living together in the same house for years."

"That's not news; they haven't been talking for 40 years or more."

Weird, thought Jay. He was getting bored already. Seemed like C.C. was too. His face was hidden behind a newspaper.

"Them danged Russians!" Stanley, an elderly, hard of hearing farmer with chewing tobacco juice seeping down his chin, was almost yelling. "Them Commies are going to bury us, ya know! They're everywhere and when they take us over, that'll be the end of our freedoms! Joe McCarthy was right!"

"I don't know about that, Stanley," The Big Bobber replied. "I don't think Kennedy will let them take us over." Stanley muttered something into his coffee cup.

The subject was quickly changed by Marge, a long-retired schoolteacher. "Kids these days! I don't know what's gotten into them," she snorted. "Lazy, the lot of them. Shaggy hair, listening to that devil music and lord knows what else!"

She took a breath and peered at her audience. "It's not like it used to be in the good old days, when we were kids! Things have changed!" she targeted C.C. who was now actually hiding behind his newspaper. "Right, Clarence?"

C.C. Lowered his paper and paused a few moments. His reading glasses were perched halfway down his nose. "Well, yeah, I guess you're right, Marge. Things are different these days. Cars go faster, we didn't have any television, there were no airplanes..."

"Dang it, Clarence! You know what I'm talking about...the kids these days, getting in trouble and all!"

"I dunno, seems like even back then we could get into plenty of trouble. Didn't you ever get into any trouble when you were younger, Marge?"

"Absolutely not!" Nora snorted, turned away from C.C and proceeded to ignore him. C.C. went back to his newspaper. Jay was trying hard not to laugh.

The talk changed to crops, weather and parking problems on Main Street. C. C. put down his newspaper and after the coffee and the grape Nehi were finished, they bid everyone goodbye and headed out the door. Marge glared at C.C and did not say goodbye.

"I think she likes you, Clarence," The big Bobber said, "don't you think so too, Jay?"

C.C. frowned and Jay laughed.

They stopped back at the Wishy-Washy Laundromat; their baskets of clean and folded clothes were waiting for them. The woman had already left, as had the loud family. They put the baskets in the Buick's huge trunk. "You could put one of them little Volkswagons in this trunk," The Big Bopper bragged.

At the Wakanda Trading Post, they were greeted by Darlene, who was smoking a cigarette and standing behind the cash register. Darlene Klabunde and her husband Dewey had opened the store after world War

II; staring out as a small neighborhood grocery, and recently expanding in size and hours. The two of them ran the store with the part time help of a couple of high school students, who stocked the shelves and carried bags of groceries to customers' cars. They were trying to give it the feel of a larger supermarket, while keeping the small-town atmosphere of a neighborhood grocery. They still had a ways to go. The store included a butcher section; Dewey cut the meat. Doris handled the books (ordering, money in, money out). They shared cash resister duty.

The three shoppers split up when they entered the store, taking two lists and two carts. As the other two headed down sperate aisles, Jay wandered over to the large rack of magazines, paperback books and the two area newspapers. As he did every week, he paged through a few magazines: Field and Stream, Popular Mechanics, MAD, JC Whitney catalogs. There were some mens' magazines with evil looking Nazis torturing women in bikinis on the cover. (Jay didn't think he should be paging through those). He moved on to the paperback books; many of them Westerns. He selected one and joined C.C. and The Big Bobber, who were talking to Dewey over by the meat counter.

Dewey was cutting up pork chops and lecturing. "The town's being taken over by hoodlums on motorcycles," he told them. "God, it's awful!"

"Is that right?" asked C.C. "Don't recall seeing many motorcycles around here."

"Trust me. I've seen three this summer already; hoodlums in leatherjackets on them. Smoking cigarettes." Jay glanced at Dewey's full ashtray by the butcher block. A half-smoked cigarette smoldered in it.

"Anyway," Dewey continued, "I was thinking about going over to Caroline's Billiards one of these nights and shoot some pool, if I can get one of these kids who help out around here to stay later and help Doris close up. Want to go sometime?" he asked.

"Sure, Dewey", C. C said. "We'd be up for that".

"Can I go?" Jay asked.

"Don't see why not," The Big Bobber answered. "We can teach you a few things about pool."

Four bags of necessities (and three 8 packs of Bullfrog beer) went into the Buick's Volkswagen-sized trunk.

Lunch then followed at Millie's Diner. It was getting crowded; mostly downtown workers, trying to order and eat and get back to work, all on a too-short lunch break. Everything and everyone seemed rushed.

After eating, C.C. leaned back in his chair and lit an after-lunch Chesterfield. "Sure am glad I'm retired." He blew a smoke ring. "Nowhere to go and all day to get there."

"Yeah, me too," said The Big Bobber, "but some days I don't feel like I get much of anything done."

"But there's always tomorrow…or next week…or next month." C.C. blew another smoke ring. "Besides, a wise man once said when you're retired, every day's Saturday."

Last stop before heading home was always Caroline's Billiards Hall. A few glasses of Blatz beer, a few games of pool and a visit with Caroline and her husband John completed each weekly trip into town. Caroline's name was on the sign and she was usually around, on one side of the bar or the other. John, a WWI veteran and semi-retired farmer, was usually behind the bar. He had traded in his doughboy uniform for a new "bar uniform" of white shirt and white apron, which matched his grey-white crew cut.

The billiard hall was filled with a number of elderly men. Jay was by far the youngest one there-by many decades (maybe even centuries, he thought). They were lined up at the bar and on benches that circled the four large billiard tables in the back. Some talked, most smoked, all were watchful. The pool players, as well as the spectators on the benches, seemed serious and very intent. Johnny Cash walked the line on the jukebox.

Two twenty-something young men sat at the bar. They both had a little longer than usual hair. John, in his no-nonsense manner, checked IDs. Satisfied that they were of age, he poured them each a glass of Blatz. A little later, after he learned that they had recently been honorably discharged from the Navy, he even bought them each a beer.

"Look at that" C.C. observed. "Old John never buys anybody a beer." He ordered two glasses of beer and a grape Nehi. "You buying for us too, John?"

"Hell, no!"

The Big Bobber took a sip of beer. "If you don't start buying, me and C.C may just start going over to the VFW instead of giving you all our business. Besides, they say there's a new woman bartender there, more friendly and much better looking than you."

"Go ahead, break my heart. That'd be two less old men I need to babysit on Tuesdays."

"Hell, John, you're older than both of us."

Talk turned to fishing. Per John, bluegills were biting, walleyes not, northern were biting, trout not. He always heard a lot of fishing stories in the bar-some true, some not and John always seemed to have a pretty good idea of what was going on in the fishing world-and where.

Several beers, a couple of grape Nehis and several games of pool later, they headed back to Hoot Owl Hollow. Big Bobber had won a little over two dollars playing pool; C.C. had lost the same amount.

After unloading the car and putting their purchases away, C.C. and The Big Bobber each took a couch on the screened-in porch for a quick nap. Jay took his new cane pole and a few worms to put underneath his new bobber and headed to the lake in search of some eating-size bluegills, the fishing talk at the bar on his mind.

5

Crawler Hunting and Trout Fishing

The opening day of trout season was always the first Saturday of May. "The time for the amateurs," The Big Bobber would say. They never went out on opening weekend. "Too crowded."

Today was June 5th and Jay had finished eating supper some time ago and was reading a paperback western on the couch. C.C. and The Big Bobber were outside, walking around the yard with flashlights. It was getting dark.

"Jay!' The Big Bobber called, "Come on out here and bring that empty coffee can that's on the cupboard."

"Why?"

"Just come out. We'll show you."

Jay grabbed the can and came out by the brothers. The lawn was wet. It hadn't rained but the hose was out and it looked like the lawn had just been heavily watered. C.C. and The Big Bobber seemed to be looking for something in the wet grass. Lost keys, Jay guessed.

"Hold out that can," C.C said as Jay came to them. Three or four large, wiggling nightcrawlers were dropped into it.

"We're hunting nightcrawlers," announced The Big Bobber. "Getting bait for tomorrow morning!"

"What's happening tomorrow morning?" Jay asked.

"Trout fishing!" C.C. answered, "you'll get to see The Big Bobber actually use a cane pole.

The Big Bobber added several more big crawlers to the can. In the beam of the flashlights, Jay could see that the lawn was covered in them. "I don't get it," he said, "why are all the nightcrawlers in the yard?"

"Because we brought 'em out," The Big Bobber replied. "See, we get the ground real wet with the hose and the crawlers don't like a lot of water so they come to the surface, especially after dark. We spot 'em with a light and scoop them up before they can scoot back into their holes."

"Can I try it?"

"Sure," C.C. said. "I'll hold the light for you."

Jay grabbed for a crawler but it sped back into its hole before he could catch it.

"You gotta be faster."

Jay tried again. This time he got a good hold on one before it got too far into its hole and started to pull it out.

"Ease him out. Don't pull too hard or you'll break him in two. Easy does it."

Jay did as he was told and tossed his first nightcrawler in the can.

Before too long, they decided they had enough bait and retired to the front porch. C.C. added some damp, shredded newspaper and dirt to cover the crawlers.

"Trout fishing in the morning; let's get going by 4," said C.C.

"Yeah," the Big Bobber agreed. "We want to be on the river by dawn. Better get to bed soon. We need to sleep fast. 4 am will come quick enough."

By 5 am, after parking in a nearby field and navigating fences, downed trees and underbrush, they were at the Sugarbush river. The sun was on its way up; it was a calm, quiet morning. There was no one else around. "Perfect," said C.C.

At his insistence, all three had cane poles rigged with no bobbers, a couple of split shots, a hook and a whole crawler. The Big Bobber moved a little bit downstream and C.C. stayed by Jay.

"Always watch the water," he said. "Watch the seam where the faster water separates from the slower water. Usually at a bend or around structure, like a rock or something. Trout often sit in the calmer water and wait for their food to drift towards them especially if its warm out. They don't like to work too much when its warm. Look for deeper holes where fish may be stacked up. They also like the outsides of the river bend and hide under overhanging brush and undercuts on the banks. They like the cover and shade. Cast upstream and let your bait drift down; maybe even a little under the overhang if you can do it without getting yourself snagged up."

That's a lot to remember, thought Jay. He'd lucky to remember any of it, but he'd give it a try. He swung his cane pole out and let the bait fly-right into a branch hanging directly overhead.

"Oops."

C.C. reached up and untangled the line. "Keep trying but keep the tip of your pole lower. And don't cast like you would for other fish. Cane poles aren't made for overhead casting. Plus, there's too much brush and too many branches that can get in your way. Just keep the rod lower and flick the line out, off the end of the pole, easy-like and let the current move the bait."

Jay kept trying. Soon, he was not getting tangled too much in things overhead but was getting snagged by unseen things in the water. The Big Bobber came over and handed him a small bobber. "Here, put this on," he said. "Maybe a foot and a half or so up off the bait. It should help."

Jay attached the bobber and tossed his line-underhand-into the river. His bobber went down almost immediately. He quickly landed a small fish.

"Hey, I got a trout!" he announced.

"You got a chub."

"A chub? What's a chub?"

"It's a rough fish and we don't want to keep it." The chub went back in the water.

"That's ok," C.C. told Jay. "You're bound to get chubs from time to time. They're common in a lot of streams and rivers around here."

An hour later, they had caught some trout, a few browns and even several brookies and placed them on a stringer. Jay had even caught a couple trout (and a few more chubs). He also had some more snags and tangles but they were happening less and less.

They decided it was time to eat the sandwiches they had brought. C.C. and The Big Bobber shared the thermos of coffee; Jay had his Grape Nehi. After they ate, they decided to fish a little longer and try to get their limits. "We can have trout for supper, "Jay said.

"Yeah, and you can clean them. It'll be good practice for you." C.C. told him.

"Hey! Whatya think you're doin' there?" a voice yelled from behind them. An old man in overalls and a chore coat stepped out of the tree line.

"And a top of the morning to you too, Lenny," answered C.C. "What are you yelling at us for?"

"Oh, it's you guys-C.C. and The Big Bobber and whoever the young'un is," Lenny responded, squinting through his glasses. "Sorry 'bout that, my eyes ain't what they used to be."

"The young'un is Jay, our great-nephew. He's staying with us this summer. Not a bad kid but he has a lot to learn about fishing and such."

"Staying with you guys, huh? Poor kid," said Lenny. "He has my sympathy."

"Lenny owns that farm over there," The Big Bobber told Jay. "This is his land and he don't like trespassers, but he doesn't care as long as its us. Right, Lenny?"

"Yeah, you guys are ok. But I've been having trouble with kids from town. They come out at all hours in loud cars, with girls, drink beer and usually leave a mess. Sometimes they party late at night. I kick them out but they keep coming back. The sheriff don't do nothing, even though they're trespassin' and litterin'. Says he can't catch 'em."

Lenny shook his head and sat down against a tree. "Guess I'll just sit here a bit with you guys. Maybe I'll help Jay with fishing tips; he needs a better teacher than you two."

Even though he was getting better, Jay continued to get snagged more than he would have liked. He lost several hooks and crawlers to branches-both on the shore and under the water. However, his three elderly coaches helped him with advice and his snags continued to lessen as the morning passed.

By 10 am, they each had their limit of nice sized trout. Lenny had left them sometime earlier. He'd been sitting against the tree one minute; Jay had been watching the river and looked back the next minute and Lenny was gone. Instantly. "Where'd he go? I didn't see or hear him leave."

"Lenny's like that," The Big Bobber said. "He can sneak in and out without a sound. He was a game warden back in the 40's and early 50's. Snuck up on a lot of violators in his day."

"He had some good tips about fishing. I learned some things from him," Jay said.

"Yeah, well," replied C.C., "he knows his stuff; almost as much as we do."

They took their stringers of fish and headed back to The Big Bobber's Buick. As they got to the car, The Big Bobber cussed. "Sonofabitch!"

"What's wrong?"

"My keys. I locked them in the car."

"Use your extra set," C.C. said. "You just bought extra car keys the other day."

The Big Bobber glared at him. "They're back at the house!"

C.C shook his head and mumbled something to himself. Jay stood there with a simple solution on his mind. "You could break the little driver side vent window and reach in and get 'em."

"Break a window? I'd couldn't ever do that! Not to my Buick!"

"What else you going to do?' asked C.C. "Got a better idea?"

No answer. They all looked at each other, looked at the car and looked back at each other. The Big Bobber finally took a deep breath, walked out into the field and came back with a baseball-sized rock. The vent window shattered, the keys were retrieved and they climbed into the car with their fish.

"Let's stop up by Lenny's house and we'll give him a couple of trout for dinner,"

C.C said.

The Big Bobber didn't say a word all the way home. C.C. wisely kept his mouth shut. Jay sat in the back seat and thought about the strange relationship between some men and their cars. "At least we got some nice fish," he offered.

There was no response.

6

Visiting and Visitors

Most of the old brothers' friends were also elderly; at least the ones they socialized with. They never referred to it as socializing. It was 'visiting.'

There were several forms of visiting: having other people over to their house, going to others' houses or going to a restaurant, tavern or some other public place and using the telephone. 'Visiting' participants could include family members, friends, acquaintances and strangers.

Jay was encouraged to go along with them on their visits. "It'd be good for you to meet some more of the folks around here," he was told. Sometimes Jay didn't like going along; other times, he didn't mind it. It depended on who they were visiting and how interesting the visit would be.

Jay usually liked it when they visited their male friends. Sometimes they would meet at Caroline's Billiards for an hour or two of pool. Sometimes they would meet in the morning at Millie's Café for coffee. Jay didn't go along at those times; they always met the guys too early in the morning for him. Other times they would meet at someone's house for cards.

The mens' topics would usually involve many of the things Jay was interested in: fishing, wildlife, cars, current events. Jay often felt that he learned a little something from these visits. Sometimes, the visit would include a beer or two (grape Nehi for Jay). He noticed that at those times, the discussions got a little livelier. The discussions would also usually include old stories of long-ago exploits; things they had done, places they'd been, what they had seen. Many tales were both interesting and funny, but Jay suspected that more than a few of them may not be totally true, either intentionally spiced up or had become a bit hazy and a little less accurate over time.

Sometimes, C.C. and/or the Big Bobber would visit elderly women, usually Norma (The Big Bobber's idea) or Abbie (C.C.'s idea). Jay didn't like these visits much; they were boring, unless Norma's or Abbie's respective grandchildren were around. The beverage of choice of these visits was always coffee and the topic of conversation was usually local gossip about other peoples' comings and goings. After several of these visits, Jay would come up with excuses to not go and before long, C.C. and/or The Big Bobber would usually let him stay back at their house if he didn't want to go because other kids wouldn't be there.

Playing cards was a popular past time; sometimes with just men; sometimes with both men and women. With the men it was often poker. In mixed company the games included Gin Rummy, Hearts, Spades and Euchre. Money often changed hands at the poker games, but it was always small amounts and sometimes matchsticks were used instead of coins. Beer and cigarettes were often involved in the poker games but usually not at the coed card games.

The brothers didn't use their telephone all that much. It had been installed a couple of years earlier and was on a party line which meant many neighbors used the same line. This resulted in much eavesdropping; others on the line could listen in on their neighbors' conversations. The party line was major source of entertainment and news for many people. It was not unusual to hear the tell-tale signs that nosy neighbors were on the line during a phone discussion. Of course, everyone with a party line knew of the lack of privacy and most folks were used to it. Some didn't care if someone was listening in, others were careful about what they said and some others would get angry. Of course, if anyone was asked outright if they ever eavesdropped on the phone, they would always deny it.

The local newspaper, a weekly, always included a section that noted who was visiting who. The visitor or guest (or both), would notify the paper of the visit and it would be printed. (Mr. and Mrs. John Doe were the guests of Mr. and Mrs. Jones on Thursday). This section, along with the weekly obituaries and police reports was very popular with the readers.

One evening, C.C. came home early from a visit with Abbie. Jay and The Big Bobber were sitting on the front porch. The Big Bobber was drinking a Bull Frog Beer; Jay a grape Nehi. "You should have come with me this evening," he told Jay. "Jackie and Jo were there unexpectedly. They asked about you. They sat with us for a bit but you could tell they were bored. Told them they should come over and see you, but Abbie said it was getting late but Jackie, of course, disagreed. Abbie said no to them but that you should stop over tomorrow."

The next day, right around noon, Jay was sitting at Abbie's kitchen table; Jo across the table from him and Jackie to his right. Abbie was serving up big bowls of macaroni and cheese. "Take all you want," she said, "but eat all you take. Children are starving in Ethiopia, you know."

"Where's Ethiopia?" Jay asked.

"Not sure, maybe in southern Illinois; by St Louis or something."

After lunch, Abbie bustled around the kitchen, cleaning up. Jay and the girls sat at the table. They offered to help but Abbie said no; she was almost done.

"It's a nice afternoon out; too nice for you three to sit inside," she said. "Why don't you children walk down to the Busy Bee drive-in and get yourselves some ice cream? Here's some money. And please being me back a couple of chocolate bars." Visiting in the house was ok and Abbie was kind to them and well-liked, but the kids would rather be outside every chance they could get.

Sometimes, visitors showed up unexpectedly at Hoot Owl Hollow; especially in the summer. Who they were and what they wanted determined the type of reception they received. Sometimes known acquaintances dropped in, 'because they were in the neighborhood'. If the brothers had the time to visit, they didn't mind unless it was someone they didn't care for. Other times, strangers would come around; some looking for directions, some had the wrong address and some were trying to sell something.

One day, Jay answered the door and two attractive, older girls in t-shirts and shorts stood on the front step; each were holding some magazines in their hands. A shiny new Chevy SuperSport idled in the driveway behind them.

"Hi, handsome. We're selling magazines to pay for our college education. Can we sign you up for some subscriptions? It's a real good deal!" They showed him some of the covers of magazines they were holding: Field and Stream, Car Craft, Hot Rod, Outdoor Life, Hot Rod Cartoons.

Jay was hooked. "Sure! Uh, how much?"

"Only ten bucks per each year-long subscription. It's really good deal but just good for today only and you have to buy at least three subscriptions."

"Ok, I'll take Field and Stream, Sports Afield and Hot Rod Cartoons." He thought about asking them about comic books but he didn't want to look like a little kid.

"That'll be thirty bucks and we can only take cash. Sorry."

"Ok, just a minute." Jay went back into the house to find C.C.

"Can I get an advance on money I'll be making this summer to buy some magazines?" he asked. "I've found a really good deal!"

"Is that so?" C.C.'s eyebrows went up. "Magazines, huh? How much?"

"Thirty dollars."

C.C. stood up. "Stay right here," he told Jay. He went out the front door.

Jay stayed right there. He heard loud voices outside and the slamming of two car doors as a car with a loud muffler sped away. C.C. came back into the house.

"Did you get my magazines?" Jay asked.

"Let me explain something to you. That was a scam; a con job. Those girls were just going to take your money and you would have gotten no magazines except for maybe a couple of the outdated old copies they showed you."

"How do you know? They seemed real nice."

"Yeah, real nice," C.C. said sarcastically. "I know because we've gone through this before. The same girls were around here last year and got money off a bunch of good, local folks, mostly young men and boys. I'm surprised they came back again this year."

"Oh." Jay felt stupid.

"You're probably feeling stupid. Don't. A lot of older, otherwise smart people have fallen for their tricks."

"Yeah, I suppose you're right."

"Think of it as a learning experience. Look, I'll buy you a couple of real magazines when we go into town later this week."

C.C. headed for the telephone. "Now, I have to give Big John, the constable, a call and tell him that they're back. This time I got their license number."

7

The Mighty Musky Hunter

I t was late afternoon; calm and quiet on the lake. A few birds could be heard in the woods along the shore line and a dog barked in the distance. Jay sat in the middle seat, between C.C. in the stern and Fisherman Andy in the bow. "What are we fishing for again?" he asked.

"Muskies!" Replied Fisherman Andy. "The state's most famous fish!"

"Whatever we can catch," muttered C.C.

C.C., dressed in an old lightweight army jacket and wearing a local feed mill cap, was securing a long nightcrawler to his cane pole. He started to drag the crawler near the bottom of the lake, behind the drifting boat.

Fisherman Andy, on the other hand, looked like an ad out of a very stylish outdoor gear catalog: new fishing vest, new sunglasses, new straw fishing hat with a green, semi-clear visor. He held a large rod and reel with line that looked to be the size of baling twine. A huge artificial lure, the size of a small submarine, was tied to the end. A large fully loaded tackle box sat at his feet, taking up most of his foot room.

Jay spotted something in the tackle box. "What's the gun for?" he asked, pointing to the small .22 revolver sticking out of from under numerous, lures, extra line, bobbers and sinkers.

"You have a lot to learn about musky fishing, young man".

Jay knew a musky fishing speech was going to follow.

"Muskies are big, with sharp teeth. They'll take down birds, ducks, small dogs and even take a man's hand or foot clean off if they're so inclined. And If you hook one, sometimes the only way-the safest way-to get it into the boat is to shoot it. And if you get it into the boat you have to protect yourself from it going after you with those teeth. "You gotta have a gun handy." Fisherman Andy stopped for a breath

C.C. rolled his eyes and snorted. "You don't need a gun to catch a musky."

"Maybe not to catch it but sometimes it's necessary to help land it and be safe with it in the boat."

"You'd shoot it in the boat?" Jay asked. He thought about bullets going through a fish and continuing through the bottom of a boat. "Sounds like a real bad idea."

"Sounds stupid. A .22 has a range up to a mile," C.C. added. "It could mess up a boat pretty good."

"Oh yeah? Never happened to me!"

"How many Muskies have you shot?" C.C. asked

"Well, uh, none. Haven't had to yet."

"How many muskies have you caught?" Jay asked Fisherman Andy.

"Never kept count," Fisherman Andy snapped.

C.C. snorted again, but this time added a "huh."

"So how do you catch a musky anyway?" Jay asked.

"The best way is to slowly row along, trolling and dragging the bait along the bottom," C.C. responded. "Nightcrawlers work fine with a long strong rod like this one." He held up his cane pole. "Otherwise, you could use large sucker minnows under a huge bobber, like The Big Bobber does. That works pretty well for him."

"Bull crap!" This from Fisherman Andy. "The wily musky is the fish of a hundred casts, or maybe a thousand; I forget which. But Muskies are best caught on big artificial musky baits. They're specially designed to catch the big boys." Jay eyed the packages of new (and many as yet unused) musky baits overflowing Fisherman Andy's tacklebox.

"You mean these big lures that weigh so much and cost so much and may or may not actually work?" C.C. asked.

"They're worth it." Fisherman Andy heaved his small submarine lure as far as he could out into the lake. It hit with a loud splash, sending ripples out the size of small tidal waves. He reeled it in slowly. When it came near the boat, he moved his pole around in a figure-eight pattern before reeling it all the way in.

"What was that for?' Jay asked.

"That was a figure-eight."

"Why?"

"Sometimes, when a musky follows a bait, it may not hit until its close to the boat. The figure-eight move keeps the bait in the water a little longer, and gets the fish agitated enough to grab it."

"Does it work?"

"Sometimes."

C.C. snorted. "Sucker minnows and nightcrawlers are the answer to musky fishing."

Andy bristled. "Artificial is the only way to fish."

"Not on your life," C.C replied. "Live bait it is. Your way is unnatural."

And so the argument started and continued way too long. Jay quickly tired of it and wished he was back at the house, or anywhere other than stuck sitting between the two "experts."

Suddenly, "Hey! Oh, man!" C.C. was holding a seriously bent-over cane pole. The line was tight and his bobber was out of sight.

"What do you have?' Jay asked.

"Gotta be a monster musky!"

"Probably just a snag," offered Fisherman Andy.

"No snag pulls back like this." C.C. pulled but couldn't get the line to move up.

"Don't horse it!" counseled Fisherman Andy. C.C. just glared at him.

"What the hell?" The line was slowly moving and so was the boat.

"Wait, I'll get the gun!"

"Are you nuts? What are you going to shoot?" asked C.C.

"Get it to the surface and I'll let him have it!'

"Is that even legal?' Jay asked.

"Get it to the surface? I can't move it at all!" C.C. held tight and the fish and the boat kept moving.

"Don't horse it," Andy said-again. C.C. just glared at him-again.

It all went on for 30 minutes before C.C. announced, "I'm getting tired."

"I'm getting bored," said Fisherman Andy, still holding his .22.

"Hell with it." C.C. started tugging on his line, trying to force it up and closer to the boat. A tug of war started but it was a short war. Snap! The line went limp and C.C fell backward into his seat.

"What happened?' asked Jay.

"Snapped the line. Lost it; took me in the weeds. Sure felt huge. A monster. Maybe a trophy."

"Never knew muskies to bite on a crawler," muttered Fisherman Andy. "Must have been a trophy snag or maybe a trophy snapping turtle," he added, putting his .22 back in his tackle box.

It was starting to get dark and they started thinking about going back in. Other than C.C.'s mystery fish, they had no other bites, no strikes, nothing.

As they neared the pier, Jay could see a couple decent sized bass along the drop off. "Look! Bass! Maybe we could shoot these fish."

C.C. laughed. Fisherman Andy gave Jay a dirty look and didn't say anything.

8

Meeting with the Governor

C.C. honked impatiently from his loaded down International. The bright red truck was filled with boxes, bags, a couple bald tires, some scrap lumber and other junk. Today was 'Dump Day' and C.C. was waiting on Jay. "Let's get goin!"

Jay ran out of the cabin, clutching a cased .22 rifle and a full box of shells. "All set." He closed the door and C.C. rolled out of the rutted driveway in low "granny" gear.

Going to the dump was a regular and a very important part of the routine of Hoot Owl Hollow. Every Thursday morning (unless it was raining or other bad weather; then it was any other day-except Tuesday, which was "Going-Into-Town Day", or Friday afternoon-which was "Going-Visiting-Day", or any other day when fish may be biting, or Saturday afternoons or Sundays, when the dump was closed), they'd load up the truck and head down to the county highway which took them to a town road, which took them to a gravel road, which took them to a dead end road named-of all things-'Dump Road', which led right to the Muckawini town dump.

You could take just about anything and everything to the dump: paper, tires, cans, bottles, wood, metal, all kinds of stuff…except junk cars, trucks and other big iron equipment. All that went to O.C. Grady's Junkyard (with free pickup within 30 miles), which was always another adventure.

The dump was run by wiry, toothless, gray bearded Mr. Everett Fisch who presided over it as if it was his own personal domain (which it kind of was, even though it was owned by the township). He, along with this wife, Verna and their adult daughter Rosie, was always on site during open hours open (weekdays 8 to 5) and Saturday mornings (until noon). The dump was only open on Tuesdays, Thursdays and Saturday mornings in the Winter. When it got cold, Verna and Rosie usually stayed home.

A small shed served as their 'office.' Verna and Rosie would usually sit outside, under a large tarp for shade, on discarded lawn chairs, while Everett prowled his domain. The shed was surrounded by piles of discarded treasures: furniture, tires, scrap metal, lumber, and numerous other items, many unidentifiable. There were some separate sections for specific things but a lot of the trash was dumped over a ridge into a large area below. Most of the trash was just that-trash-but there were always some items that could be repaired and even some that were still usable.

Everett called everyone "Sirs" (men, women and children) and he liked to be called "The Governor." The Governor never sat down; he was always on the move. He greeted everyone personally; and made a point of directing them to the assigned drop off spots for their trash. "No! Sirs, the refrigerator goes over there and the wood over here! Here, Sirs, I'll take the sofa, just put it over behind the shed. Hold on Sirs, that old ironing board looks good, set it there too." And so on.

The Governor was the boss.

The Fisch collection was legendary. They lived in an old farm house a couple of miles from the dump and at the end of each day they would load up their old flatbed Ford and haul a load home. Their house, sheds, barn and yard got fuller by the week; most of their treasures came from the dump, but some locals who knew where they lived would often drop off 'donations' at their house. Most of the items were unusable but some were repairable and some things were functional; occasionally a few antiques of some value showed up.

Although the only things not accepted at the dump were junk cars, trucks and other large implements and equipment, those restrictions were more lax at the Fisch house. A few rusted-out farm implements, junk cars and non-running trucks rested in the yard, waiting for O.C. Grady to come pick them up and pay the Governor for the scrap metal.

Verna and Rosie rarely moved from their chairs but would smile at the 'customers' and talk to the locals when they were approached. Today, they had a transistor radio playing Polka music.

"Things have changed," C.C. told Jay. "People will throw everything away these days. They don't bother fixing stuff like the old days, just toss it out and buy new stuff. These dumps are a big business."

As C.C. pulled into the dump, the Governor waved. "G' mornin' to you, Chief!"

The Governor began calling C.C. 'Chief', which was his shorthand for fire chief, just after C.C.'s had bought his bright red truck.

"Mornin', Governor!"

"Got anything good on board for me today?"

"Not much, just junk but have yourself a look." The Governor helped them unload the truck, tossing most of the trash. However, several new items were added to the Fisch family collection.

Even though the Fisch family always reserved the right of first selection of anything that was brought in, the Governor was often generous to his friends and would allow them to take things that he or Verna or Rosie didn't want. Strangers and people he didn't like would not be allowed to take anything. He considered C.C. to be a friend and therefore, C.C. was known to frequently return home with things form the dump. So far, he hadn't ever brought back a bigger load than he had gone to the dump with, but he came close at times. Today, an old dresser (missing only one drawer), a (according to him) repairable lawn chair and a non-running lawnmower were loaded onto C.C.'s truck.

When they were done, Jay brought the .22 out of the truck cab.

"Bad news, Chief," the Governor said. "Can't shoot no more at the dump. Town Board says no more shooting. Want me to put signs up."

"What the hell?" C.C. asked.

"I dunno. Maybe someone complained. Maybe they don't want no more rats killed. Who knows? I heard the local NRA chapter is pissed and there's talk about a lawsuit against the township for goin' against the 2nd commandment, 2nd attachment or something like that. Say that people have the right to shoot at the dump. I hope the town doesn't get sued though; I'd probably lose my job if that happened. Or at least get my pay cut."

"Darn it." Jay had wanted to shoot at some cans.

"But I'll tell you what," the Governor told them, "go back down that road there about half mile and there's a trail that goes back to a little, old gravel pit that ain't used no more. Don't know who owns it but nobody is ever there. There's no signs that say keep out. I figure it'd be ok to shoot in there. Don't guess anyone would mind."

"Thanks," said C.C. "We'll go check it out."

They soon found the abandoned gravel pit. Like they were told, there were no signs and no one was around. Targets could not include any animals, birds, anything glass but cans were ok. C.C. made sure they picked them up and took them with them.

"Seems like you're getting a little better," C.C. said. "But got to keep practicing."

And Jay did. From then on, every trip to the dump included a side trip to the little gravel pit and Jay killed cans. No one ever complained.

Except for The Big Bobber. He regularly complained every time they returned when he saw the 'treasures' C.C. would bring home. "More junk!' he would grumble, shaking his head.

9

The Art of Bluegill (and Other) Fly-Fishing

"Fishing may be a sport to some folks but fly-fishing…fly-fishing is an art!" Leechman proclaimed to Jay and Harvey.

The boys had stopped at the bait shop for some worms for the blue gill fishing they had planned for later that afternoon. Leechman had caught Jay eying the fly-fishing gear that he had put on display. "Interested in fly-fishing?" he asked.

"Don't know. Never tried it. Seems complicated."

That started a mini lecture on fly fishing. "Not really. It's not complicated at all, once you know what you're doing. But it is different. Anybody can dunk a worm in the water and maybe catch a fish. But fly-fishing takes skill, finesses and a lot of knowledge."

"Knowledge of what?" Harvey asked.

"Lots of things: the water depth, movement and temperature, the make-up of the river or stream, where the fish are, what they'll hit on, what the hatch is and when it is, the weather, all kinds of things."

"Sounds pretty much like what someone needs to know for regular fishing."

"No, no. Its different. You boys should try it. I know you'll like it. Once you try it, you'll be hooked." He chuckled at his poor joke.

Two weeks later: "I hate it!" Jay was standing along the banks of the Wolverine River. He and Harvey were both standing with loops of fishing line spooled around their feet.

They had taken Leechman up on his offer to take them fly-fishing. He had lent them each a fly rod set up with line, leader and tippet; he had even put a Wooly Bugger, his favorite lure, on both of them. "If you can get this out to where the fish are and work it correctly, I guarantee you'll catch yourself trout."

Jay scowled and carefully reeled in the line that surrounded him. Leechman continued providing advice and guidance. "Don't try casting it like you would with a regular spinning rod and reel," he counseled. "It doesn't take a lot of strength. You don't have to heave it out as far as you can, as hard as you can. Distance is often good but precision and placement and presentation are the most important."

Leechman caught several nice trout; neither of the boys got anything. His casting demonstrations made it look easy, which added to the boys' frustration.

Harvey moved farther downstream. He moved slowly as both he and Jay were wearing borrowed chest waders that were too big for them. "Cast over to the far bank. I'll bet trout are hanging around that dead tree in the water," Leechman advised.

Harvey decided that he had a better chance of casting far enough to reach any fish that might be there if he got closer to the other bank. He started across the river, half shuffling, half stumbling. After only a couple of yards, there was a shout and then a big splash. Harvey's head and shoulders were above the water, the rest of him submerged. The fly rod was still in his hand. He struggled to stand up and slowly rose to his feet. He was standing in about 3 feet of water and soaked to the bone. "My waders got water in them," he yelled, "and it's hard to move."

"Come on back over here and for heaven's sake, be careful!" Leechman yelled back to him. Harvey slowly inched his way back. Once on dry land, he sat down, took off his waders and poured the water out of them.

"Well I guess that's the end of today's lesson," Leechman announced. He inspected Harvey's waders. "One thing to learn is to have the right soles on your waders for the river you're fishing. These are rubber soles. They're slippery. These waders should have felt soles on them. That's my fault. Another lesson to learn is to be careful and go slow when moving in the water. Also, always watch for rocks, logs and holes, especially holes that you may not be expecting."

As they headed home, Leechman said, "You guys should get out to the middle of Muck Lake in the boat and practice as much as you can. You'll have more room and less things to get hung up in.

"Muck Lake?" Jay asked.

"You know, Lake Muckawini, Muck Lake," Leechman replied. "That's what I've always called it."

Leechman continued, "And practice in your back yards. When you can cast your lure into a coffee can 60 feet away from you, you'll know you are a fly fisherman."

"That'll be the day," Harvey muttered.

In the weeks to come, the boys spent as much time on Lake Muckawini with new fly rods they had bought at the Coast to Coast store. Jay's reel had the line spool enclosed and you pushed a lever and it wound up the line. They felt their casting was getting better. They kept Leechman's words in mind: 'Don't heave the line.' 'Let the line do the work." "Bring your casting forearm straight up, don't let it go behind you, pretend there's a wall back there.' 'Don't flick your wrist, keep it a smooth motion'. 'Mend your line.'

That's a lot of stuff to remember, Jay thought. He still wasn't very good yet but he felt he was getting better.

On a Wednesday evening, Jay and Harvey fished for bluegills (or whatever else would bite), using their fly rods and surface poppers. They could see insects landing on the water surface.

"Must be some sort of hatch. Hopefully, there'll be some fish interested in these poppers." Jay said.

There were. Along one of the lake's many reed beds, they both caught several small bluegills right away. They anchored and over the next half hour they caught more 'gills; a few of them keeper size. Those went on the stringer that Jay carefully tied to the boat before putting it in the water.

Jay was reeling in a small bluegill when, the water exploded and the small fish disappeared under the surface. Suddenly, a large bass broke the surface with the bluegill in its mouth.

"Wow! Set the hook!"

"I'm trying, but I can't; the hook is in the bluegill's mouth and the bluegill is in the bass's mouth."

The bass took off took off and headed back into the reeds. The line snapped.

"Do you believe that? I never saw that before."

"Me neither," Harvey agreed. "It was really cool but no one will believe us."

They fished a little longer, until it was almost dark and then they headed in.

Later that night, after supper, Harvey returned to Hoot Owl Hollow and he and Jay sat outside at the picnic table. "Well, I told C.C and The Big Bobber about the bass and bluegill," Jay said. "You were right, they didn't believe me."

A week later, the boys were on the lake again. This time, Leechman had taken an hour or so off and to join them to continue their lesson. "Can only stay out here for a little while," he told them. "Les is running the bait shop and I don't want to leave him in charge for too long."

Over the next hour, they tied on mayfly caddis and blue winged olive nymph flies. Leechman had them try different flies and explained the importance of matching the lure with the hatch. Some were productive, some not.

A few fish were caught but not by Jay. He was getting skunked. "Here, look at this." He brought out a small jar filled with soft kernels of corn.

"What are you going to do with that?" Leechman asked.

"I was telling Uncle Tom that we were learning fly fishing. He said to put a kernel or two of soft cooked corn on a fly. Says it really works."

"What?" Leechman shook his head. "No way. That's an old rumor that has no basis in anything. These flies here are the best lures to use, without corn or anything added to them. A good fly fisherman would never use corn!"

After a little more time passed without Jay catching anything, he snuck two kernels of corn on his fly and casted it out when Leechman wasn't looking. He soon landed a small bass.

"Good job," Leechman said. "Told you that that fly would work and you didn't need to put any corn on it. Jay didn't tell him that he had.

Jay kept adding corn and kept catching fish. After he had taken his fourth fish off of his line, Leechman caught him rebaiting with corn. "What are you doing? I told you that corn doesn't work."

"But it does. I've caught all of my fish so far with corn."

"I'll be darned. Let me see that jar of yours." Jar passed the corn jar to Leechman, who put a kernel on his hook.

Several weeks later, C.C. said to Jay, "We're going to have some folks over for a fish fry tonight. You and your friends want to go get us some bluegills for supper? We have some in the freezer but we could use some more."

So Harvey, Jay and Jackie headed out for bluegills. Harvey took his fly rod and poppers and wooly buggers. "I really want to get good at this," he said. Jackie and Jay took spinning reels and angleworms and wax worms.

The sky was overcast and the weather forecast called for showers, but not until evening. They figured they had a couple of hours to fish before the rain started. This should be a good time to fish.

They started out along the reed beds along the shore. Nothing happening. They worked along the drop off for a ways. Nothing happening. They rowed over to the public swimming raft and casted alongside of it. Jackie and Jay caught a couple of bluegills but the fishing was pretty slow going. They then moved back close to the shoreline and the drop off. Harvey casted in towards the reeds. He was using a Wooly Bugger. "Leechman said the Wooly Bugger is a good all-around lure," he said. "I'm sticking with it for now."

Overhead, the clouds were getting thicker. "We better watch the weather," Jay said. Everyone agreed.

They continued to slowly work their way out past the drop off into deeper water. "Let's head over there," Jackie pointed. "I think the water gets about 30 feet deep, but there's point that comes up to about 4 feet and I've heard that it's a good spot." Jay didn't bother asking her where she'd heard it. Jackie was always hearing things about fishing spots and she was usually right. She was getting to be like a younger version of Fisherwoman.

About five minutes later, Jackie yelled, "Stop! This is it. She pointed down to the water. It had gotten shallow; they could see weeds and the lake bottom. Just as they casted, raindrops started falling. "Rats. We better go in."

"No, wait," Jay said as he pulled in a nice bluegill. Let's see what we have here."

Harvey took the fish and put it on the stringer, made sure it was tied to the boat and put it into the water.

Jackie looked up at the sky and then scanned the horizon. "Ok, it's raining but no thunder or lightning. If you guys don't mind getting a little wet, we can stick around a while as long as there's no lightening." So they stuck around. The rain got heavier (still no lightning) and they started catching fish. It was like someone threw the fish biting switch to 'on.'

The rain had gotten much heavier. Water started building up in the boat, to the point where Jay had to start bailing with a large coffee can, kept in the boat for that purpose. They soon caught their limit of nice bluegills; the Wooly Bugger and wax worms worked especially well. They had a stringer full of fish, were soaking wet but happy. They slowly headed in to shore; Jay rowing and Harvey bailing.

C.C. looked up from the newspaper he was reading when the three of them came in. They stood there, soaking wet, disheveled and looking very unhappy. "Holy smokes," he said. "Look at you guys. I was getting worried. I knew you didn't have the sense to come in out of the rain, but also knew you were smart enough not to stay out there if it was lightning. Did you catch any fish for us?"

'Yeah, we got a nice bunch of them," Jay said quietly.

"You don't sound very excited about it. Where are they?"

"Well, yeah, we caught a lot of bluegills but we don't exactly have them or have all of them now." Jackie especially looked uncharacteristically unhappy.

"Here's what we have left," Harvey said as he pulled the stringer from behind his back. On it were the heads of a lot of nice bluegills but their bodies were mostly chewed off.

"What the heck happened?"

"As near as we can figure," Jackie said, "when it started raining, some turtles decided they were as hungry as the fish were. Sometime between the time we put the last fish on the stringer and we pulled the stringer out of the water at the pier, turtles, or maybe northerns or bass, were dining on our catch."

"I guess that means no fish fry for us tonight," Jay said.

C.C. shook his head and grinned. "Guess we'll just have hotdogs instead."

10

Night Fishing Isn't for Wimps

Harvey, Willie, Jackie and Jay loaded the 14-foot boat with lifejackets, tackle boxes, fishing poles and a collection of flashlights and other lights. They needed a lot of light; they were going night fishing. The boys had never done it before. Jackie said that she had done it a time or two, so she was considered the guide. His grandma had insisted that Harvey bring his little brother along with them. "And make sure you make him wear a life jacket!"

"The lake at night is pretty cool," Jackie said. "It's quiet out here and sometimes you see neat and weird things and hear strange sounds in the woods. If you don't let that spook you, you'll like it."

Their arsenal of lights included two medium sized flashlights, a Coleman lantern and Jackie's big, powerful spotlight.

"The big difference is that we're fishing more by feel than by sight. After you cast, pinch your line between two fingers. When you get a bite, you'll feel it right away," Jackie told them.

Jay rowed out onto Lake Muckawini. Jackie was right; it was quiet, almost too quiet. The water was calm and there was a sliver of a new moon rising. They followed the drop off as best they could, moving along the extended reed bed between them and the woods. They set the lantern on the boat's middle seat. It gave off light in the boat and to the edge of the reed bed but it couldn't illuminate anything under the water.

Jay immediately started hearing sounds. Farther out in the lake, they could hear an unseen fish jump on the surface somewhere away from them. But more there were also sounds coming from the woods beyond the shoreline, out of the lantern's glow. Owls were loudly hooting at each other. Every once in a while, they could hear some movement in the woods; twigs snapping, leaves rustling. Nothing to worry about. Possums, raccoons and deer, he told himself.

Suddenly, a fairly loud crash in the dark woods startled them.

"What was that?"

"Not sure, but probably a deer," Jackie said. "Or a bear," she added.

"A bear?" Willie was concerned.

"Maybe, but probably not."

"If it is, we're safe out here on the water, right? Bears can't swim, can they?" Harvey asked.

"I've seen pictures of Polar Bears swimming and I bet their southern cousins can too," Jay told him.

"Bears swim?" Willie was more concerned.

There were no more crashes or loud sounds but Jay kept a nervous eye on the shoreline any way. He rowed the boat into deeper water, a little farther off shore.

With worms as bait, they started catching a few bluegills, but the fishing action was slow. Harvey got snagged on something under the water and had to break his line. Tying a new hook on was a challenge in the dim light. Jay got a backlash and Jackie hooked a tree when she casted too close to the shore.

They weren't using bobbers because it was too hard to see them. They caught a few more suspended bluegills and a few perch that were sitting right on the bottom. They didn't let Willie cast his own line. Harvey put a bobber on his line and did the casting for him, figuring there'd be less tangles and snags that way.

Jay was reeling in his line when he felt a strong tug. He set the hook. "Hey, I have a fish. Good sized, I think."

"Don't horse him," Jackie counseled.

"I'm not and I won't! This feels little funny he's fighting but…". Jay worked the fish up to the boat and they got a look at it. It's a decent bass," Harvey exclaimed, as Jay brought it part way out of the water.

"You snagged it!" Jackie laughed. "Look at that, your hook is stuck in the top of its head."

"What the heck? How did that happen?" Jay answered his own question. "The hook must have snagged him when I was reeling in."

They unhooked the fish and gently let it go.

Before too long, Jay fought with another snag as Jackie tried to untangle another backlash. The lantern was getting dimmer; the fuel was running out. Before too long, they had 8 panfish between them but they had also had double that many snags, tangles and backlashes.

"This night fishing is a pain," Harvey grumbled.

"Yeah, it's getting frustrating," Jackie agreed.

"I don't know why we aren't catching more fish," Jay complained.

"It's because we're spending most of our time untangling backlashes or breaking our line off on snags," Jackie answered.

"Where are all the fish?" Jay wondered as he took the powerful spotlight and shined it down into the water. A medium sized northern looked up at him. "Hey, look at this!"

Jay gave the light back to Jackie and slowly rowed the boat along the shoreline, staying in the shallower water. They watched as other fish came into view. Mostly bluegills, but some perch and bass.

"This is great. And we don't have to worry about snags or anything."

As they rowed on, they could see dogfish, schools of minnows, another larger northern and some more smaller fish. A few small box turtles showed up in the light. Suddenly, a large snapping turtle slowly cruised by under the boat.

"Wow!" Just look at those! We should try to catch a turtle or two," Willie suggested.

"Why? What would you do with a turtle?

"Put it in a fish tank or something and keep it as a pet."

"Who keeps a turtle for a pet?" Jackie asked.

Willie admitted he didn't know anybody who did. "Or we could get a big snapper and make turtle soup out of it.

"How would we handle a big snapper?" Jay asked.

"You don't know how to make turtle soup," Harvey told Willie.

"Well no, but I could learn. Can't be too hard. Hey, look down there!" Willie pointed down to the weeds on the bottom.

Jay aimed the spotlight. They watched as a lone crawfish shot backward as it was hit by the light. Jackie then pointed over to a nearby patch of weeds on the bottom. "They're in the weeds and there's more of them!" Numerous crayfish stirred and tried to hide in the weeds to avoid the light.

"Maybe we can catch some," Willie said.

"For what?"

"To keep as pets."

"Not again, Willie," Harvey scolded him. "Who has crayfish for pets?"

"I think some people eat them," Jay said.

"Yuck!" Jackie made a face. "Doesn't sound too appetizing to me."

"We could make crayfish soup," Willie exclaimed.

"No, we aren't going to eat any of them. But sometimes, they're used as bait for bass and other fish," Jay said. "I read about that in Field and Stream."

"How would you catch them, anyway? They're right on the bottom and they can move really fast."

"Maybe with a small net a with a long handle."

Jay continued silently rowing. Suddenly they heard the faint sound of twigs snapping and some slight splashing of water on the shore. They shined the flashlight in that direction and saw a doe and her two fawns drinking at the edge of the water. They had been interrupted by the intruders and now they stared wide-eyed into the beam of light.

"We better let them be." The flashlight was shut off and they immediately heard more twigs snapping as the mother and her youngsters disappeared back into the woods.

The owls, who had been quiet for a while, started hooting again. "The owls are neat but they sound sorta spooky," Jay said.

"Scared, Jay?" Jackie asked.

"No, but I'm nervous about bears," he answered. And bears and coyotes and wolves and wild dogs and big snakes and rabid racoons and spiders, he silently added to himself. "I just hope we don't run into any bears," he said aloud.

"Bears?" Willie was concerned again, his eyes wide.

"Boys, there aren't any lions, tigers or bears around here," Jackie assured them.

It was getting late so they headed back towards home. Jackie was looking up in the sky. "Stop a minute. Look up there!"

"I don't see anything but stars and a little moon," Harvey said.

"I saw a shooting star. Look! There goes another one!"

They all saw that one. After sitting for about ten minutes, they saw three more. Then another small point of light started moving slowly across the sky above them. Suddenly, the light grew larger and brighter.

"What is that?"

"Don't know."

"It looks like its getting closer to us."

"Sure looks strange. Is it a UFO?"

"Bet its a space ship," Willie said.

"No, probably just a high-flying plane."

"Doesn't look like plane. It's moving too slow and planes have more lights."

The light suddenly disappeared. "That was quick," Jackie said. "Where'd it go?"

"I'm scared!" Willie announced.

Jay quickly started rowing back to their pier. They saw a couple more shooting stars by the time they tied the boat up, but no more signs of the strange light.

C.C and The Big Bobber were watching TV when Jay and his friends came into the house.

"Catch anything?"

"Yeah, a few."

"Get any tangles or snags?"

"Yeah, a few.

"Only a few?" C.C. chuckled.

"Ok, quite a few. But we saw some really neat things on and in the lake. And shooting stars in the sky and, oh, one UFO."

C.C. and The Big Bobber raised their eyebrows. "Only one?"

"It was a big spaceship," little Willie told them. "Full of Martians. It came right down to us!"

"No, it didn't come right down to us," Harvey said. "And we didn't see any Martians. But it was weird looking."

The Big Bobber and C.C. just smiled, shook their heads and went back to watching TV.

11

Riding with the Warden

"I was thinking," Warden Jim said. He and C.C were sitting at the truck stop, each with a cup of coffee in front of them. "Jay seems like a good kid and seems interested in the outdoors. Do you think he'd like to go out with me for a couple hours on patrol some night?"

"Can he do that?"

"Sure, we call it a ride-along. Community relations. Don't do it much but we can offer it to interested people. I especially like to take young people who might want to see what warden work is like."

"Dangerous?

"Not at all. If we get into some trouble, I take measures to endure his safety."

"Lots of red tape?"

"No, I just need a parent sign a form that it's ok and agree not to sue the state or me."

"A parent? They're both a long way away."

Warden Jim thought about it a minute. "Well, I suppose I could let you sign off as 'the responsible adult.'" He chuckled at his last statement.

"I think Jay would love to do it. Wouldn't hurt to have him get a look at how the good guys work.'

"Flattery will get you nowhere, at least with me. Save it for Abbie."

Later that afternoon, C.C. found Jay on their pier, practicing his fly casting. It wasn't looking too good. "How's it going?" he asked.

"Terrible. I'll never get the hang of this. I may as well give it up."

"Not too long ago, you said the same thing when you were learning to cast an open-face spinning reel. But now you've gotten pretty good at that."

"This is a lot harder."

"Naw. Its just different." C.C. lit a cigarette. "I had coffee with Warden Jim this morning and he said that you could go on a ride-along with him if you want."

"What's a ride-along?"

"Well, it's when you go out with the warden and get to see what he does for a living. Check licenses, look for violators, all that stuff."

Jay thought long and hard about it; for about 5 seconds. "That'd be neat! When can I go?"

"I'll talk to him and we'll get it set up."

Three evenings later, Warden Jim pulled into the yard at 7pm. Jay was eagerly waiting. He climbed into the dark green unmarked sedan, moved a clipboard off the seat and tried not to disturb the various papers, maps, binoculars and other items that filled the car. "Thanks for letting me come along," he said.

"It's my pleasure. Thought you might like to see what wardens do. We have several things on our to-do list for tonight. We're scheduled to be at the library at 7:30 to briefly meet with some folks who are working on a history of some of the area lakes. They have a few questions for me and want to schedule a time when I can come and give a longer presentation on how fishing around here has changed over the years. Then, we have to go and talk to a farmer who wants to charge his neighbor with trespassing on his land. After that, when it's been dark for a while, we will probably be setting up in a couple of areas where I've had reports of deer shiners. Unless something else comes up"

"Cool. Are we going to arrest anybody?"

"No. 'We' aren't going to do any such thing. As a matter of fact, if we get into a potentially tense situation, I'll have to drop you off in a safe area for a little while."

"Darn."

The library visit was boring but it was short, as Warden Jim had said it would be. He was scheduled to return the next month for a longer meeting.

They then took a ride out to a farm, seemingly in the middle of nowhere. The owner obviously had been waiting for them; he met them in his driveway. "It's about time you got here. I've been waiting."

"I apologize, sir, "Warden Jim said. "We got here as quick as we could."

The farmer told them his name was Mr. Hannum and that that his neighbor, 'a young whippersnapper', was always crossing over his fence and coming onto his property. The property in question was a large fenced-in field that stood between the two houses. "I yell at him to get off my land. He always just waves at me and then leaves but sooner or later he comes back and does it again."

"How often does he go into your field?"

"Maybe every few days, when its nice out. Sometimes more, sometimes less."

"Does he do anything to or on your property? Take anything? Wreck anything? Have you ever talked to him about it?"

"Looks like he picks something up and takes it with him but he's a ways away and I can't see too good that far. And no, I ain't never talked to him. Doubt it would do any good."

"Ok, I'll check it out. I'll go talk to him and see if we can straighten this out.'

"I want him arrested!"

"I'll see what I can do."

Jay rode with Warden Jim to the accused's house but was told to wait in the car. "Just in case," he was told.

As Warden Jim got out, a tall man came out of the house, followed by a little boy. They stood near the car; Jay could hear them talking. A woman also came out of the house and another younger boy watched from a window. The man introduced them as the Borski family. Warden Jim introduced himself. Mr. Borski told him that they had moved into their new home several months ago and he, his wife and two young sons loved living in the country. No, they hadn't met any of their neighbors yet but were looking forward to doing so when they had the opportunity.

Warden Jim explained the purpose of his visit; that their neighbor had accused him of trespassing and asked Mr. Borski about him going into the neighboring field.

"Well, I often play ball with my boys. Sometimes the ball isn't caught or is hit or thrown where it wasn't intended to go; once in a while it may go a short ways into the field. I only go into the field to pick up the ball and leave right away. It's only a few feet in and I never thought it'd be problem. Never thought of it as trespassing. Sorry about that. Once in a while I do see my neighbor over there. He's a distance way when he comes out and he yells something to me and waves. Can't clearly hear or understand what he says and I thought he was just being friendly."

"I'm not sure it's a wave; probably more like shaking his fist," Warden Jim said. "You should go talk to him and not do it anymore."

"I'd be happy to talk to him." Mr. Borski paused. "But would you go over there with me?"

Warden Jim, Mr. Borski and Jay headed back to speak with Mr. Hannum. Warden Jim acted as mediator and explained both sides of the situation. Mr. Borski said he would make sure he didn't come on his neighbor's land without permission and the two neighbors shook hands.

"Just stay outa my field," Mr. Hannum said as they left. So much for mending fences between them.

Next stop was a neat little cabin set back in the woods in the northern part of the county. Warden Jim pulled into the yard and honked his horn to announce his arrival. "Don't need to sneak up on these folks; they asked to meet with me and report a bear that's been getting into their garbage and attacking their bird feeders."

The cabin door opened and an old man came out. His wife followed behind him.

"Evening Warden Jim."

"Evening, Frank," Warden Jim replied. "Got some bear trouble, huh?"

"Yep. Gets into the bird feeders. Wrecks them. Gets into the garbage, strews it all over the yard. Seen him a couple times in the evening; big guy. I'm getting fed up with it. Ready to shoot it."

"You don't want to do that. How long has this been happening?"

"A couple weeks now."

"Any cubs?"

"Nope, haven't seen any."

"Did it seem to come after you or threaten you or the Missus?" Frank shook his head. "You don't have dogs, do you?" Frank again shook his head.

"This happen before?"

"Oh, yeah! Off and on for years."

"How long did it go on in the past years?"

"Not that long. Back then, it only lasted a couple weeks. Seems like he's staying around this time."

"My guess is that at this time of the year, your bear is moving through, just visiting the area. Probably hungry and hanging around for a while because of the pickings here. They do that. Unless he stays on and keeps it up or you feel you're personally in danger, there isn't much we can do at this point. Let's take a look at your garbage cans and feeders."

After a quick walk-through of Frank's yard, Warden Jim said. "You may want to do a couple of things. First, secure the lids of your garbage cans and move them into your garage, behind a closed door. Second, stop feeding your birds and put the feeders away for a few days. Your bear should lose interest and move on.

"I don't want to stop feeding the birds," Frank protested.

"It'd be only for a little while. They'll be ok. Its summer and your birds can find plenty more to eat. If your feeders are gone, they'll find other food. When you put your feeders back out, they'll quickly come back to them and you can then keep on feeding them. Birds have good memories like that. Besides, the birds won't eat if the bear is hanging around the feeders."

"See how that works," Warden Jim continued. "Try it for the next several days. If the bear sticks around and causes any more problems for you, call me right away and I'll come back. And for Pete's sake, don't shoot it!"

"What if it comes after me or the missus?"

"Well, then I guess you'd need to protect yourself but shooting it would be the last resort."

It was after dark as Warden Jim and Jay left Frank's cabin. "We'll check out a couple boat landings and then head over to a farm west of Wakanda. The owner has called in reports of someone poaching deer after dark."

There was nothing going on at the two boat landings; no parkers, no partiers, no violators, no problems, no nothing. They moved on.

Thirty minutes later, Warden Jim pulled into a dark farmyard, shut off his lights and positioned his squad car between a tractor and a hay wagon. They were facing a large field; there was a town road running along the far edge of it. "We'll just sit here awhile and see if anyone shows up. The owner knows we're going to be hiding here," he added.

They sat listening to Warden Jim's radio. 'If something happens and I have to go after and chase someone, I'll have to leave you here," he said. "Don't worry, it's a nice, warm night and you'll be ok until I get back."

"Oh?" Jay was nervous. He was thinking about Frank's bear.

Warden Jim noted Jay's worry. 'I'll tell you what. If I have to go, I'll leave you a flashlight and my handheld radio, ok?"

"OK, I guess so."

They watched the field. No lights. They watched the road. Several cars went by but none of them stopped. They were just getting ready to leave when a car came down the road and stopped.

"Oh-ho!" Warden Jim put his powerful binoculars to his eyes. "Car's stopped and a guy's getting out. No light or gun yet, but… wait! Oh good grief, he's taking a piss on the side of the road."

Jay laughed. "And he doesn't know we're back here watching him."

"Nope, he has no idea we're here. Thinks he's all alone."

"Wow!" said Jay. "That's…I don't know if it's neat or scary that he has no idea we're watching him."

Warden Jim saw no sign of a spotlight or anything else to be concerned about. The guy finished his business, got back into his car and drove away.

"Well, I think that's enough for tonight," Warden Jim announced. "I'll drop you off at Hoot Owl Hollow and head home to bed myself. "Hopefully, my radio will be quiet for the rest of the night."

Once home, Jay was getting ready for bed when The Big Bobber stuck his head in the doorway.

"You're still up?" Jay asked.

"Yeah, I was visiting the outhouse when Warden Jim pulled in. How did it go?"

"It was really neat! Those wardens respond to a lot of people and things and they can be really sneaky," he said.

"Yeah," agreed The Big Bobber. "That's their job; it's what they do. I'm going back to bed. C.C. and I want to hear all about it, but in the morning but now it's time to sleep." The Big Bobber left for his bedroom.

12

The Working Boys

It was explained to Jay that there were 'chores' and there were 'projects.' The chores were those day to day tasks that Jay was expected to help out with; keep his room relatively clean, help with dishes, help with the infrequent house cleaning, take out the trash on a daily basis and burn it in the big burning barrel.

Projects were bigger, supposedly time-limited and almost always involved more work than chores. Jay was assured that he would be paid for any help he would provide on the projects; one dollar an hour. Minor projects could include raking, mowing and helping to repair various things.

Both C.C and The Big Bobber were really good at coming up with major projects.

The Brush Clearing Project

One day, C.C. decided that they needed better paths through the woods. Three existing paths were targeted for widening and cleanup. He consulted with the Big Bopper and they summoned Jay. "Here's a chance for you to make some money. Cutting and clearing the brush along those trails and stacking it up in several big piles. It's a sizeable job so maybe you might want to ask some of your friends to help you."

Jay asked his friends. Harvey was the only one interested. "Sure, I could use some money."

The paths were fairly long and winding. It took them most of the week to clear the brush to the brothers' liking. They made five large piles of brush between the driveway and the boat house.

"Looks good," C.C. told them. "Now, maybe you could rake and mow the trails."

"More work," Jay grumbled.

"More money," Harvey said.

A couple of days later, they were finished. The Big Bobber was sitting on a lawn chair when they approached him. "Here come the working boys," he greeted them. "Suppose you'd like some money."

"What are you going to do with the brush piles?" Jay asked as he put his money in his pocket.

C.C. came over and joined them. "Haven't decided yet. Maybe burn them this winter. Or haul them back farther into the woods for shelter for some of the smaller animals."

"They'd make good fishing structure," The Big Bobber said, "but getting them into the lake would take quite a bit of work. Plus I'm not sure if it's even legal to do that anymore".

After C.C. and The Big Bobber went into the house, Harvey said to Jay, "You know, you're right. Those brush piles would make great fishing structure. We could put them in the lake ourselves and not tell anyone else where they are. We'd have our own hotbed of fishing action."

"Yeah, that'd be cool. We'd tie them up as tight as we can and sink them. There are some broken concrete blocks behind the shed we could use for weight."

"And then, we could haul them out after dark in the bigger boat and toss them in without anybody seeing us."

They realized that they'd have to tell the brothers what they were going to do. "That'll be fine with me," The Big Bobber said. "Knock yourselves out and don't get caught."

C.C. thought about it for a minute, then nodded. "Just make sure you sink them deep enough so they aren't a hazard. And don't get caught."

It took them two nights to get the job all done. As they came into the house after their last trip out on the lake, they were greeted by The Big Bobber. "So you're all done, huh? Did anyone see you?"

"Nope, we were really quiet and careful."

"Good. Now all you two have to worry about is remembering where you dropped them."

The Dump Truck Projects

Too late, Jay realized that calls that his great uncles had been making to the JV Trucking Company would mean another project and more for work for him.

It started when C.C. announced: "We need to do something about this lawn. The grass isn't growing very good in this sandy soil."

"Yeah," The Big Bobber agreed. "A load of black dirt would make a difference."

"And fertilizer and grass seed and water," C.C. added.

Later that week, Jay watched as a huge, fully loaded dump truck with the JV Trucking Company sign on the door, pulled into the yard.

The truck driver was a big guy in a cowboy hat and smoking a cigar. "Where do you want me to dump it?" he asked C.C.

"Right there." C.C. pointed to the middle of the yard. When the truck was empty, the driver pulled out of the driveway and a small mountain of black dirt stayed behind.

"Here's a chance for to make some money, Jay." C.C. told him. "All this dirt needs to be evenly spread over the whole yard. It's a sizeable job so maybe some your friends would help you. We'll pay."

Jay asked his friends. Harvey, Jackie and Les all volunteered.

"So, four of you. That's good; it'll go quicker. We have a couple wheelbarrows. You'll also need shovels and rakes. The Wheel Horse and its little trailer could be of help. Use it if you want." Of course, Jay wanted to.

For the next several days, the four friends worked hard for 4 hours each morning, before the day got too hot. They were able to spend much of their afternoons in or on the lake, fishing or swimming. Before too long, they had all of the dirt spread around the yard. They were proud of their work.

C.C and The Big Bobber inspected it. "Looks good. Next, we add the fertilizer, mix it in with the dirt and then sow grass seed on it."

"We?" Jay asked.

"I meant you."

"Oh. More money for us?' Jay asked.

"More money," he was told.

"And then," C.C continued, "it'll have to be regularly watered on days we don't have rain."

"More money?" Jay asked.

"No. That'll be an ongoing chore for you."

Two weeks after the yard had been fertilized and seeded, the same JV Trucking Company dump truck came up the driveway. The Big Bobber met it when it came to a stop.

"Where do you want this load?" the driver asked; a cigar again in his mouth.

"Over by the lake; next to the boat house."

When the truck pulled away, another small mountain, this time of yellow sand, remined behind.

"What's that?" Jay asked The Big Bobber.

"Sand."

"I know that. What's it for?"

"To make it nicer for you kids to swim off the pier and firm up some of the real marshy areas by the boat house."

Oh, oh, Jay thought, here it comes. "It'll have to be spread, right?"

"Right. Here's a chance for you to make some more money. It's a sizable job so maybe some of your friends will help-for pay, of course."

Jay asked around. Harvey, Jackie and Les were willing to help.

"It'll be nice not having it so mucky around the pier when we want to get in the lake," Jackie said.

"Yeah. And nice to have some more extra money," Harvey added.

They moved sand with wheelbarrows and spread it with shovels and rakes over the marshy areas along the shore. They also dumped some in the water along the pier to make a strip of the lake bottom more solid for wading. They were careful to leave enough areas untouched and keep the weeds and other natural cover for small fish, snails, crayfish and other wildlife. As before, they only worked in the morning and but they worked hard and were done in several days.

When they were finished, the four of them surveyed their work. "Looks pretty good if I say so myself," Harvey said.

"You mean if *we* say so ourselves," Jackie corrected him. "It'll now be much better getting in and out of the lake."

They walked back to the yard where C.C. and The Big Bobber were sitting. "Here come the working boys," C.C. said, pulling out his wallet.

"And one working girl," Jackie added.

Three weeks later, the same big dump truck again pulled into the driveway. This time, it looked like it had a full load of pea gravel. C.C. and Jay were sitting outside. "Oh, no," Jay said, "not again!"

"Where do you want this dumped?" The driver put a fresh cigar in his mouth.

"Drop it all in a pile beside the driveway, about halfway down. We'll take care of it from there."

Jay watched from his lawn chair. "We?" he muttered. "I don't think so."

The truck left and C.C walked over by Jay. Before C.C. could say anything, Jay said, "I know, more spreading. More money. Shovels, rakes and wheelbarrows. Would you put the snow blade on the Wheel Horse? Could we use it to spread gravel?"

"Yes to all of that," C.C. responded. "Good idea. I'll put the blade on the tractor this afternoon. Better see if you get help again."

This time, only Harvey volunteered to help Jay. The rest of the kids were too busy or something.

It took Jay and Harvey three mornings to get the driveway covered with a new layer of pea gravel. They hooked the little trailer to the tractor, loaded it with gravel and, after dumping it, used snow blade to spread it out. It was still hot and heavy work.

After looking over the completed job with the boys, The Big Bobber pulled out his wallet. "Good job, guys."

"Anymore dump trucks coming?" Jay asked him, afraid of the answer.

"Nope, that should do it."

Jay relaxed.

"For now, anyway," The Big Bobber added.

The Painting Project

"Fisherman Andy asked me if you'd be interested in painting his garage for him," The Big Bobber told Jay. "Said he'd pay a dollar an hour; I told him I'd ask you.""

"Maybe." Jay thought a minute. "His garage isn't all that big but it needs some scraping first. Scraping is a pain in the butt. I wouldn't want to do it by myself; would need to see if I could get some help. And I'd want $1.25 an hour."

"Wow, you're getting to be a regular businessman. I'll tell him all that."

Jay talked to Harvey. "I'm not that enthused about painting and it would take a while which leave us less time for fishing and other stuff," Harvey said, "but ok. I could use the money."

Les also agreed to help. Linda said she didn't like to paint. Jackie and Jo couldn't; they'd be gone for the next two weeks.

Fisherman Andy reluctantly agreed to the pay increase. The boys went over to his house right away so he could show them how he wanted it done. The white garage was peeling and it would need some scraping but it wasn't as bad as Jay thought it would be.

Brush and bushes were tight up against the garage. Heavy in spots. "That'll all need to be cut down, grubbed out and raked up before you paint," Andy told them. "And make sure you spread a tarp on the ground to catch the scraps of paint you guys scape off."

"Man!" Jay muttered. "Looks like a lot of extra work; more than I expected."

"More money," whispered Harvey.

"Paint, brushes, a ladder, tarps, saws and rakes are in the garage," Fisherman Andy told them. "I'll be gone for a few days," he added. "You can start anytime you want, but the sooner, the better. I'll leave the garage unlocked."

The long-range weather forecast looked promising so they decided that they would start the next day. The next morning, they met at Fisherman Andy's house. They brought sack lunches and several cans of soda. Fisherman Andy was getting ready to leave and told them he would be back on Friday. "I hope you can have it all done by then."

They worked hard, cutting brush and putting it in piles. "What are we supposed to do with the piles?" Les wondered.

"I don't know," Jay replied. "I'll ask C.C. what he thinks."

"I hate, hate, hate raking and grubbing out bushes!" Harvey grumbled. He took a break with a lukewarm bottle of soda. "And it's getting hot out."

"Let's try to get this over as quick as we can; hopefully today."

They all cut, raked, piled and sweated. Harvey grumbled. They took frequent breaks in the shade, but they were making good progress.

"We should have brought our swim trunks; we could take lake breaks," Jay said.

They finished cutting and piling brush that afternoon. Later they met back at Hoot Owl Hollow and cooled off in the lake. "Just leave the brush piles," C.C. had told them. "Fisherman Andy can decide what he wants to do with them when he gets back."

The next day they returned to the job site with their sack lunches, sodas and swim trunks. They scraped all morning.

"I hate, hate, hate scraping!" Jay grumbled. "let's get this section done and then we'll stop for lunch."

As they worked on their sandwiches and sodas, Harvey asked Les what kind of sandwich he was eating.

"A Rueben that my dad made for me. Has corned beef, sauerkraut and swiss cheese. It's my favorite."

"Man, I can't even look at sauerkraut without having to crap," Jay said.

They went back to scaping. Suddenly Les said, "Oh, no! I have to crap, bad! Must have been the sauerkraut."

"What are you going to do? The house is locked."

"Not sure but I'll figure it out." Les went onto the garage. "Ah ha!" Minutes later he came out with an orange clay flowerpot. It looked to be full and was covered with an old dirty rag.

"Did you just do what I think you did?"

"Yeah, nature called-loudly. I had no choice." He headed toward the lake.

"What are you doing?"

"Destroying the evidence." Les threw the full flowerpot as far as he could out into the lake.

They finished scraping that afternoon. "Let's put on our trunks and swim.'"

"No way! Some of Les's crap is out there somewhere in the water."

They put their equipment in the garage and headed back to Hoot Owl Hollow.

The next day, they started painting in the morning. Later, they ate their lunches by the lake. A breeze was pushing small waves against Fisherman Andy's pier.

"What's that?" Harvey asked. He pointed to something colored dull orange bobbing out in the water, slowly moving towards them on the pier. As it came in closer, they could identify it as Les's flowerpot from yesterday.

"Crap!" Les said.

"No crap!"

"What do you mean, no crap?"

"No crap. It's empty."

They looked closer. It was clean as a whistle. "Where's the rag that was on it?"

"Hopefully on the bottom of the lake, getting cleaned off."

They finished painting that afternoon. Saturday noon, Fisherman Andy stopped by Hoot Owl Hollow. Jay, Les and Harvey were sitting outside.

"Got it finished, I see. Good job cleaning out the brush. I'll have someone haul it away. And nice paint job. Too bad it's the wrong color."

"Wrong color? We painted it white!"

"Yeah, I wanted it painted green."

"But it was already white. White paint was right there. Figured you wanted the same color."

"I had a can of green paint in the garage."

"We didn't know. You didn't say green!"

"Well, maybe I didn't say specifically." He thought a minute. "Ok, you did the job but because of the screw up, I think I should only pay you each a dollar an hour.

"But we agreed on 1.25.!"

Just then, C.C came out. He'd heard the voices being raised. "What's up?"

Jay explained it to him as Harvey and Les nodded their agreement.

"Is that right, Fisherman Andy?" C.C. asked. "You didn't tell them what color to use? How were they supposed to know?"

Fisherman Andy backed down. "Maybe not. I guess not. OK, $1.25 it is. Let's settle up." He pulled out his wallet.

"By the way," he said, "there was an empty flowerpot on the shore, down from the pier. Don't understand what it was doing there. Do you guys know anything about it?"

"No!" Les answered quickly. "Didn't see any flowerpot anywhere around there."

13

Crappies, Chum and Turtles

Jay, C.C., Uncle Tom and Fisherwoman were sitting around the kitchen table finishing their coffee. Jay was finishing his grape Nehi. The plan for today was to fish for crappies. At least that's what Uncle Tom and Fisherwoman announced.

"Fisherwoman is the area's foremost authority on crappie fishing," C.C. told Jay.

"I ain't so sure about that," Fisherwoman told Jay, "but I do know some places where some nice crappies hang out. Don't think I'm any kind of authority but I've caught a few in my day. We'll try one of my favorite lakes this morning."

"Nah," Uncle Tom declared. "We can try your lake some other time. I found a new spot a couple of weeks ago where the crappies are so thick you can hardly get your boat in the water."

"And where's that?" Fisherwoman looked skeptical.

"Old Joe Lake."

"I know where that is; fished it a number of times but it wasn't really what I'd call a serious crappie lake."

"It's a hot spot and I figured we'd go there today. I'll drive. Also, I have a new technique that's guaranteed to catch crappies; catch all kinds of fish as a matter of fact."

"And what would that be?"

"Wait and you can see for yourself."

They loaded up Uncle Tom's Pontiac, hooked his boat and trailer up and set out for Old Joe. In addition to his usual large collection of fishing gear, he had packed a small cooler.

"Didn't know we were staying out long enough to have lunch," Fisherwoman nodded at the cooler.

"No lunch in there. Just my new secret weapon."

They were soon sitting in the boat along the drop off on Old Joe Lake. Fisherwoman baited a bare hook with a minnow. Jay did the same at her suggestion. Bobbers were attached and casted out into the water. Uncle Tom took a mesh fish basket and put several pieces of something from the cooler into it and tied it behind the boat.

"What in the world is that?' Fisherwoman asked, watching Uncle Tom as she reeled in their first crappie.

"My secret weapon. Chum!"

"Chum? What the hell is chum?"

"Well, let me tell you." Jay knew a speech was about to start. "I learned all about it in a magazine. They use it down south to attract fish to the boat so you can catch them. Its usually made up of cut up pieces of dead fish and the scent brings the live ones running."

"You mean swimming," Jay corrected.

Uncle Tom went on. "You put your regularly baited lure out, in this case, my proven-to-be-successful sparkling jig with an artificial minnow on it and the fish will head right to it, following the scent of the chum."

"I have heard about something like that," admitted Fisherwoman, "but if I recall, it was done for saltwater fishing. Never heard of it used around here. Gotta admit, I'm pretty skeptical."

"Until now," Uncle Tom said proudly. "I think I'm the first to use it up here."

"What kind of fish did you cut up to use?"

"Well, uh, I didn't have any fish to cut up so I use some old pork chops bones and chunks of pork fat that was left over from last night's supper."

"What? I never heard of such a stupid idea. Crappies don't eat porkchops or pork fat."

"Doesn't matter, it's the smell that gets them."

"Oh, brother! I'm past skeptical now." Fisherwoman looked at Jay, shook her head and made another cast with a new minnow. She had soon caught three more nice crappies; Jay had caught two.

"How are you doing there, Tom?" she asked.

"Nothing yet, but they'll be coming. Just haven't smelled the chum yet."

Ten minutes later, Jay asked, "what's that?" He was pointing to a dark thing sticking out if the water behind the boat.

"A snapping turtle! That's his head," Fisherwoman answered. "Don't let your bait get close to it, it'll grab it and then we'll have a problem."

"And look over there," Jay pointed. Along his side of the boat he could see several small turtles.

"What in the world…?" Fisherwoman started to ask.

"And more coming toward us on my side."

Over the next several minutes, they counted at least a dozen turtles hanging around the boat. They'd reeled their lines in, except for Uncle Tom. "The fish will be coming in right behind the turtles," he announced.

The boat was drifting slowly along a reed bed with a turtle parade lining up behind them and seemed to be growing. A couple more snappers had joined the group.

"Tom! You really have to pull your line in!" Fisherwoman's voice was raised.

"Not yet. Hey wait! I have something!" Uncle Tom's line went tight and was slowly moving into closer to the reedbed.

"What do you have?"

"Don't know but it feels big. Maybe a musky or big northern."

"Don't horse him," Jay smirked.

Uncle Tom just glared at him. "Get the net ready, Jay."

As they moved into shallower water, they could make out a large shape that had stopped below the boat. Fisherwoman yelled, "It's a damn turtle, Tom! A big old snapper! I told you!" Uncle Tom looked like he wasn't sure what to do, let alone what to say to her.

Fisherwoman set her pole aside. "Here, slowly try to get him up to the boat. Jay, grab me those needle nose pliers on top of my tackle box." The big turtle surfaced next to the boat. The line was strong and kept him from snapping loose; although it would have been better for him to have snapped the line. Fisherwoman leaned over the side with the long needle nose and grabbed the shank of the big jig that was stuck in the snapper's mean-looking beak. Jay moved away as far as he could in the small boat.

With a snap of her wrist, Fisherwoman yanked out the jig and the big turtle, now free, quickly headed back to the deeper water.

"Holy smokes," exclaimed Jay. "How'd you do that? Weren't you scared?"

"Not really scared, just careful. I've done this before."

Uncle Tom looked nervous. "Time to get off the lake and go have some lunch," he said, glancing at the water behind them.

"Yeah. Start the motor and I'll take care of this mess." Fisherwoman grabbed the fish basket out of the water, opened it up and dumped the chum off the back of the boat. "Gotta finish feeding the turtles," she said sarcastically, as they headed back to the landing.

A little later they were eating hamburgers at the Wakanda truck stop. "Are we done fishing?" Jay asked. "It's still early."

"No, if you want, we can stop we can stop somewhere else. Let's go to the lake I wanted to in the first place, Flying Squirrel Lake. And no more chum!"

Uncle Tom nodded.

They were the only boat on Flying Squirrel Lake. "I've had good luck here with crappies," Fisherwoman said. "Let's see if the luck still holds. Tom, you, of course, will use what you want. Jay, I'd still suggest minnows under a bobber."

The minnows and bobbers proved to be productive. After an hour, Jay and Fisherwoman had each caught their limits of crappies, plus a few small northerns that they released. Uncle Tom caught a few, too. They had started out slow, along the reed beds but soon ran into a sizeable school of fish. On several occasions, they had doubles on; both Jay and Fisherwoman hooking fish at the same time.

Jay had never seen such fast fishing action. "Man, we're catching fish on almost every cast."

"Told you this is a good lake. Plus, we happened to be in the right place at the right time." They ran out of minnows and had to use several dead ones they found in the bottom of the boat for the last few fish they caught.

That night they had a big crappie feed. Fisherwoman stayed for supper. After supper was finished and the dishes were done, they sat around with coffee, beer and a grape Nehi, sharing stories of past crappie conquests. It quickly turned into a contest of one-upsmanship between Uncle Tom and Fisherwoman.

"It's gonna be a meeting of the Liars' Club," C. C. whispered to Jay.

Fisherwoman was telling about the times she was using two poles and had big crappies on each one at the same time.

Uncle Tom: "One time, I got a bad backlash and couldn't reel the line in and I landed a 16" crappie by hand."

Fisherwoman: "One time, they were biting so hard that I ran out of minnows and still caught them on bare jig heads."

Uncle Tom: "I ran out of bait once too and used bare hooks. Got crappies on plain hooks; red and gold worked, silver didn't."

Fisherwoman: "Caught one once on a dragon fly."

Uncle Tom: "Caught one once on a piece of cloth."

Fisherwoman: "Caught one once on a tiny bit of bubble gum."

Uncle Tom: "Yeah? I caught some once on some small tiny pieces of bread I mushed on the hook."

"Are you sure that those crappies weren't really small catfish, Uncle Tom? Mushy bread is one of your favorite catfish baits and the only non-stinky one," said The Big Bobber.

Uncle Tom continued, "And one time they were so thick, I could scoop them out of the water with a net."

"That's illegal, Uncle Tom," C.C. pointed out.

Uncle Tom paused. "Ah, no! I didn't actually do that. I just meant I could have; but I didn't!"

Fisherwoman: "One time, I caught two on the same hook!"

"How'd that happen?

"It didn't. I just made that up; just like I suspect much of this discussion was." Fisherwoman stood up ready to leave and head home for the night. "I quit and will concede the game to you, Tom."

The owls had started hooting. To Jay, they seemed to be telling the humans to go to bed so the birds could have the night to themselves.

II

Christmas School Break
(December 1963)

14

On the Hard Water

Jay's first summer at Hoot Owl Hollow ended after Labor Day when he had to return home to Mendota and start the new school year. He missed his new friends and the fun they had over the summer. Now, he was trapped in a school schedule, the days were getting shorter and the weather was getting cold. Thankfully, the school Christmas break started a few days before Christmas. Jay had 12 days of relative freedom until school would start again a few days into the new year.

His family's Christmas activities ran for 3 or 4 days; including visits from both sets of grandparents, friends of his parents and various other people. The time before Christmas was filled with a lot of baking, a lot of shopping, a lot of wrapping and a lot of decorating. It was important to his parents to have everything perfect and ready in time for Christmas Eve. Jay thought it was most important to have the presents ready. The time during the holidays included fires in the fireplace, big dinners, cookies, left-overs, more visiting and presents-a lot of presents (that took 10 minutes to wrap and ten seconds to unwrap).

This year, C.C and The Big Bobber drove down the day after Christmas to visit the family and stay overnight for a couple of days. Uncle Tom came to visit the day after Christmas, but he only stayed for the day.

The plan was for Jay to ride back with his uncles to Hoot Owl Hollow, stay for several days and ride the Greyhound bus back to Mendota the morning of December 31. He had to take the bus back because his dad had to work and didn't have the time to make the 8-hour round trip to pick him up.

On December 27, Jay was in the back seat of The Big Bobber's Buick, heading North. It was quiet in the car. "Kinda cold," he said.

"Yeah," agreed the Big Bobber, "but we've seen worse." He and C.C. then launched into 30 minutes of stories of past winters; subzero temperatures, massive amounts of snow, numerous cancellations, cars not starting, walking to school in 4 feet of snow, and so on.

"So why do we live in Wisconsin? Why not where its warm all year and there's no snow?" Jay asked.

"Because there's a lot to do are here in the winter," The Big Bobber said. "I love winter. Besides, it gets too hot in those other places."

I thought he just said he didn't like winter, Jay thought. "So what'll we be doing the next few days?" he asked, changing the subject. He had never been to Hoot Owl Hollow in the winter and wasn't sure what to expect.

"The usual," answered C.C. "Go to town, maybe the dump, do some visiting. Oh, I heard that Jackie and Jody will be around by their grandmother and Les and Linda are supposed to be coming up for few days to be with their dad."

"And," said The Big Bobber, "You'll have your first chance to go ice fishing!"

That got Jay's attention. "Ice fishing? I've read about it but never did it. Sounds cold, a lot of work and few fish."

"It's not so bad. I'm sure you'll like it."

By early afternoon, they reached their destination. About 6" of snow covered the ground. Higher banks of snow lined the driveway and the road. Snow dusted the tree branches and the large wood pile. C.C.'s truck was covered with recent snow. The little Wheel Horse tractor was in the shed, now fitted with its winter accessories of a snow blade, chains and wheel weights. It had been busy, keeping the paths around and to the house open. The big thermometer nailed to a pine tree read 24 degrees.

The blanket of snow on the ground was crisscrossed with various animal tracks. "Deer, squirrels, rabbits, dogs, maybe a fox or two," C.C. pointed out as they walked to the house.

"Your bedroom is the same as it was," The big Bobber said. Jay dropped his suitcase. The place looked pretty much the same as when he left in September.

"Still have to use the outhouse, I see," he said.

"Yeah, it's kind of a pain in the winter but the good news is that we're having some remodeling in the Spring. By the time you come back next Summer, we'll have a brand-new indoor bathroom."

"What all are you having done?" Jay asked.

"Well, the powers that be are making us put in a septic system. We're the last place on the lake with an outdoor privy." Jay thought there was a trace of pride in C.C.'s voice. "That means an indoor toilet, a hot water heater and a shower in a real bathroom. No more summer baths in the lake. We'll have to give up one of the bedrooms, but the change will be worth it."

Jay walked outside and down to the lake. The wind had blown much of the snow off some spots. Even though there were still some small drifts of snow, Jay could see the shiny reflection of bare ice in many areas. The lake looked pretty much frozen over although there were a few small spots of open water along some of the shoreline where small springs still flowed. There were a lot of tracks on the lake; animal and maybe some human, from what Jay could tell.

Out past the boat landing, a small ice fishing shack sat on the ice. It looked unoccupied at the moment. Across the lake, Jay could see several people moving around. Ice fishermen, he figured. He wondered if they were catching anything.

Later that afternoon, Jackie and Jo stopped over. The three of them talked about how school was going, what they had been doing since Labor Day and what they got for Christmas.

"We both got new ice skates," Jo said. "We brought them along, hoping we could skate on the lake."

"I didn't get new skates," Jay said, "but I brought mine along." Jay had been skating for the past 3 or 4 years. There was a small, city operated skating rink across from his parents' home in Mendota and he spent as much time there as he could in the winter, playing hockey, skating and just hanging out. He had recently switched from hockey skates to figure skates. He still used the former when he played hockey but he liked the figure skates better for general skating.

"We should be able to get on the lake easily enough. There's some snow but maybe we can clean it off a little and skate tomorrow."

It was already starting to get dark. Unlike the summer months, it now got dark as early as 4:30 and 5 in the afternoon. It seemed like winter stole half of the daylight hours from summer. Jay liked it much better when it stayed light later.

At supper, Jay asked about skating on Lake Muckawini. "Yeah, that'd be ok," C.C. said. "Just don't go too far out and make sure you keep your distance from the springs and the open water on the shore. Don't want anybody to fall in." He thought a minute. "And you can use the Wheel Horse to plow the snow away for a little rink."

The next morning, after The Big Bobber showed him how to raise and lower the snow blade, Jay plowed a better path down to the lake and then cleared the snow off an area big enough for them to skate in. It didn't take him long; there wasn't all that much snow to move. When he came back into the house, he was congratulated for not falling through the ice-either him and/or the little tractor.

Over coffee and a grape Nehi, they talked about ice fishing. "Tomorrow sounds like it should be a good day for fishing," C.C. said. "We'll plan on going out on the lake then."

"I don't have any ice fishing stuff."

"Don't worry, we have what you'll need. We have extra poles and jigs, hooks and all that. Also have a hand auger for the holes. We'll pick up some waxworms and some small minnows. We'll head out on the lake for a while tomorrow and see what we can catch."

Right after lunch, Jackie and Jo showed up. "I talked to Linda last night," Jackie said. "She and Les are around and want to skate with us. They had to go to town this morning so their dad could buy them some new skates. They didn't bring theirs with them. They'll be by later."

It was a nice afternoon for skating; sunny with temperatures in the twenties. A couple local kids, who they didn't know, showed up; they had seen Jay and the sisters skating out on the lake and wanted to join them. Linda and Les came along by mid-afternoon in their new skates. Les complained that his were too tight.

"Well, they wouldn't be if you didn't put 4 pairs of socks on," Linda told him.

"My feet get cold."

They played 'crack the whip', had races and tried to stay upright while practicing fancy moves. Les blamed his too-tight skates every time he fell. When they were done, Jackie and Jo led them to their grandma's house where Norma treated them to hot chocolate and cookies she had baked. It was a good afternoon.

The next day, Jay went ice fishing for the first time. They waited until mid-morning (to let it warm up a little bit, C.C. had said). They walked a couple hundred yards out onto the lake.

"This is a good spot," The Big Bobber announced. He and C.C. took turns drilling holes, ending up with 9 holes in about 6 inches of ice.

"Here Jay, you can help clean out the holes." C.C. handed Jay a long-handled scoop. "Get the slush and ice chunks out the best you can."

They set up three buckets to sit on. Jay was advised to put a wax worm on a small brightly colored jig. In the hole it went. The brothers also baited up their poles, dropped their lines in and sat down to wait for bites. "As you can see, we practice the 'poke and hope method' of ice fishing," The Big Bobber told Jay.

After a while, Jay got antsy. He wasn't getting any bites so he set his pole down on the ice and wandered over to check out a medium size bluegill that The Big Bobber had just pulled out. At the same time, C.C. announced, "I got on one, too!" A second medium sized bluegill was laid on the ice.

Jay walked back to his bucket and hole. "Hey, where's my pole?" He looked around. "It's gone!"

"You set it on on the ice? Bet a fish grabbed your jig and since you weren't around to grab it, it pulled your pole into the drink. It's all now under the ice and it ain't coming back!' The Big Bobber laughed.

"That's ok, I have another pole," C.C. said. "Just keep this one in your hand. Maybe that way you'll get yourself some fish."

Just then, they heard some loud noises from across the lake.

"What's that?" Jay asked. "Sounds like some lawn mowers with no mufflers."

The Big Bobber eyed two dark shapes in the distance, heading towards them. "Those are snow machines; snow mobiles, they call them. Getting more popular all the time. Don't have much use for them, myself. They go too fast and make too much noise!"

"I read about them in some outdoor magazines," Jay said, "but I never saw one up close."

"You've got to admit, though," C.C said, "one could come in handy when there's too much snow makes it hard for a guy to get around, especially to get a person farther out on a lake to ice fish."

"Yeah, maybe," The big Bobber conceded. "In some of those cases, they might be alright. Pretty soon though, guys' ll be running them up and down the roads and peoples' yards, all night long, bar hopping and getting drunk and loud."

The snowmobiles came closer and then passed by; but not that close and not that fast. The riders waved at them. They waved back, even The Big Bobber.

An hour passed. They moved from hole to hole. Jay caught a few keeper bluegills and a medium size perch. With the other fish his uncles caught, they were close to having enough fish for a couple of meals.

Suddenly, a large yellow dog ran out towards them from the shore. Jay watched it sniff around a vacant ice hole that they had drilled earlier, behind where The Big Bobber sat. Jay went back to watching his fishing line. Shortly, the dog wandered over to them, circling them and their ice holes. It was a friendly, tail-wagging dog and it was very interested in the fish they had placed on the ice to take home with them. All of a sudden, when they weren't watching, it grabbed a bluegill and ran off in the direction from where it came.

"Hey! Did you see that?" Jay yelled. "That dog just took one of our fish!"

"Son of a gun! Well, we'll never catch him. Maybe we better put them fish in a bucket in case he comes back." C.C. turned the bucket he was sitting on upright and started tossing the fish in it.

The Big Bobber pulled his line out the hole he was fishing in. "No fish here. Think I'll try a new hole." He headed over to a vacant hole behind him.

Suddenly they heard; "Sonofabitch!"

"Must be bad," C.C. remarked. "He hardly ever swears."

"That danged dog! Bad enough he stole a fish. But then he goes and craps in this ice hole that I wanted to fish in. Bet there are fish down there, too. I won't get anything out of there now!" The Big Bobber was fuming. "That's the gol-dangest thing I ever saw."

"Well, I've seen gol-danger," C.C. commented, "but I can't say that ever happened to me."

"Of course not," said The Big Bobber. "That would only happen to me!" He set up in a different hole and things quieted down. For a little while, at least.

Jay wasn't catching as many fish as he hoped he would. "Can I have two lines in the water at the same time?" he asked.

"Yeah, I think the limit's three."

Jay borrowed another pole from C.C., set it up and moved over to two unused holes that were close together. He put a pole in one and another pole in the other. 'Double the chances for fish,' he thought. Before long, the pole on the right jerked hard and was pulled out of his hand. Into the water it went. At the same time, he felt a tug on the pole on the left. He held tight and set the hook, bound to keep that pole and the fish from getting away. He started pulling it in and found that another line was wrapped around it in a tangle. "What the heck?"

He pulled it in, tangle and all, and soon the rod that had gone down the right hole came to the surface. A medium size bluegill was on that pole's hook and also snagged in the left pole line.

"Holy smokes!" C.C. exclaimed. "I've never seen anything like that before. What happened?"

"Looks like the fish hit the right pole, pulled it in the water and then got all got tangled in the left pole's line," The Big Bobber observed. "Way to go Jay, you got your lost pole back and a fish to boot."

It took a while but with a little help, Jay was finally able to get his two lines untangled. He had to cut one and that pole got retired for the day. He put a wax worm on his jig and dropped it into the water.

It was getting close to the time for them to go in when they heard, "Howdy, boys!" Warden Jim walked up behind them. None of them had seen or heard him coming.

"Hi to you, Warden Jim." They showed him their fish.

"Nice bunch of 'gills," he said. "I won't bother you guys for your licenses. I know you have them. You do have them on you, right?"

They nodded.

He stood around and chatted with them for a little while before Warden Jim said, "I better go check those guys across the lake and see what they're up to."

All of a sudden, Jay's line went tight. He hung on and set the hook.

"Hey! I have something; it feels heavier than those other ones!" They all gathered around and could see a flash of a fish in the hole, beneath the ice. Jay tried pulling it up into the hole but it was hard going.

"Hey, Warden Jim! "The Big Bobber called. "Come back and look at this!" The fish was sideways and they had trouble working it up into the hole. It looked like it was going to come up and out tail first.

"What is this thing?"

As it slowly started coming up, Warden Jim exclaimed, "It's a small sturgeon. And it's been hooked through its tail. How in the heck did that happen? What'd you do?" He looked at Jay.

"Nothing different," Jay replied. "I was just jigging and it hit my hook."

"Here, you better let me bring it up. There're a lot of things illegal about this fish." Everyone agreed it was best to let the Game Warden handle it from here. Jay passed the pole to Warden Jim and a little 14-inch sturgeon with a jig caught on its tail fin was soon eased up and out of the hole.

"Let me see," Warden Jim stated and started listing off the violations: "Its under size, out of season and foul-hooked. All illegal. This would be an expensive fish if someone did this intentionally or kept it." The fish was quickly and carefully released back into the water.

That night they had a big bluegill supper, made a fire in the fireplace and sat down in front of the TV set.

"Well, Jay, for your first day of ice fishing, you sure were able to collect a bunch of fish stories for yourself."

"Yeah," Jay answered. "It was interesting. Can we go again tomorrow?"

III

Summer 1964

15

A Stormy Welcome

Jay started his second summer at Hoot Owl Hollow the Saturday right after school let out. He was much more eager to return than he had been last year; he'd been looking forward to coming back to Lake Muckawini.

They had left Mendota by 8am. The 4-hour car trip with his parents seemed to take longer than ever. As they finally pulled into the driveway, The Big Bobber and C.C. came out to greet them.

Jay looked around. Things looked much the same as they did when he left last September; the lake, the house, the sheds, the outhouse. The outhouse? "Hey! I thought you said that this year you'd have an inside toilet and hot water.

"We do," The big Bobber assured him. "Just had the remodeling finished last month. Had a septic system put in and we're now living in the 20th century. Just haven't gotten around to getting rid of the outside privy.

"Great!" Jay said. "No more spiders in the toilet."

"Well, I believe the spiders have moved into the new bathroom by now."

"Really? "Jay's eyes got wide.

"Just kidding."

Jay noticed a large metal ring had been placed on the ground, close to the picnic table. "What's that?

"A fire pit," The Big Bobber said. "I put it in a couple weeks ago. Thought it would be nice to have fires in it when we're sitting around outside at night. And thought you and your friends would like to have a fire to sit around."

Jay put his things in his bedroom and looked the house over. The end bedroom had been sacrificed to make room for a toilet, sink, water heater and a small shower. The new facilities looked pretty good to Jay; no spiders in sight.

As his parents and great uncles chatted, he went down to Lake Muckawini and looked for fish by the pier. Several small panfish looked back up at him. A half dozen or so canoes and small boats were on the lake, as well as a motorboat that slowly moved along the shoreline. The boat landing was empty, as was the public swimming raft. Memorial Day weekend had brought a lot of temporary visitors (many had since gone home) but now that it was June, things would be getting busier around the lake quickly.

His parents stayed for a late lunch but wouldn't be spending the night. They were going to drive back as far as Wausau and visit some old friends.

After they left, Jay grabbed a grape Nehi that had been stocked for him and sat on the porch between The Big Bobber and C.C. "So what else is new?' he asked. For the next hour, Jay listened to all the latest Lake Muckawini/Wakanda gossip; some true, most of it not.

The next morning was Sunday and Jay rode with The Big Bobber in the weekly ritual of picking up the Sunday newspaper. When they returned to home, C.C. greeted them with some big news.

"The weather reporters say there's a big storm headed this way. It's coming fast out of the southwest. Supposed to hit here by noon or so."

"That's only a couple hours."

"Yeah. Heavy rain, high winds, maybe a tornado. We better get things put under cover in the shed and move the boats up on the shore."

Just as boats, chairs, trash cans and other things were secured, the wind picked up and it started to rain. In no time at all, the wind was soon blowing hard and the rain had gotten heavy.

"Hope no one was still on the lake."

"I looked but didn't see anyone when I was down there."

Through the windows on the porch, they watched the trees swaying in the wind.

"Looks like they could snap at any minute," Jay aid.

"They're pretty flexible," The Big Bobber told him. "They can take a lot."

"But only up to a point. All trees have their breaking point," C.C. added.

Suddenly there was a bright flash of lightening, followed by a loud crash. "Tree down in the woods," C.C. announced.

The storm got stronger. It became dark and they had to turn some lights on in the house. Before long, the lights started to flicker, went out and stayed out.

"No power. A tree must have fell on the lines."

"Or a transformer got fried."

"What do we do now?" Jay asked.

Neither of the men seemed too concerned. They'd been through bad storms before. "We wait it out. We'll be ok. As long as no big trees come down on the buildings, we'll be fine."

"How so?" Jay was not so sure about the 'being fine' part.

"This storm seems to be moving pretty fast. Shouldn't last real long."

"We hope," Jay muttered.

"We have lanterns and candles for light. We have a transistor radio and it won't hurt us to go without television for a little while."

"What about food. You know, cooking and eating?" Jay wasn't hungry now but figured he would be later.

"If need be, we'll fire up the charcoal grill in the shed for cooking. We've had experience doing that."

"Done it before," agreed the Big Bobber.

"What about the bathroom?" We won't have water with the electricity off to the pump."

"True, but the toilet tank is full enough for one flush. And the pressure tank will have a little water in it. And don't forget, we still have a functioning outhouse. We'll just run out there between the rain drops when we have to go."

"Yeah," The Big Bobber grinned at Jay. "And spiders get really active when it rains, you know."

"Well, thank God for the outhouse," said Jay, sarcastically.

Two hours later, after a lot of thunder, lightning and rain, the storm finally started to let up. The wind died down and the rain slowed to a light sprinkle. They went outside to survey the damage. Large puddles of water the size of small lakes stood in the yard and covered parts of the driveway. The top halves of two large pines had been snapped off, narrowly missing the roof over the porch. Two other large trees and several smaller ones had come down in the woods and along the road. One looked like it had fallen over the road, just past the driveway. Down by the lake, a large tree branch had fallen on the 12-foot wooden rowboat that had been turned upside down on the shore. Another large branch had fallen alongside the shed where the Wheel Horse tractor was stored. The little tractor escaped unharmed. Twigs, leaves and branches covered much of the ground. One bird feeder was missing.

"We've got a lot of cleaning up ahead of us," C.C. said, looking around.

"Yeah, but we've seen worse." The Big Bobber tried to sound positive. "Besides, other than the boat, nothing got seriously wrecked. The house, the big shed and the boat house are intact. This is gonna take the chain saw, rakes and a lot of energy and time. Jay, you've got a chance to make some spending money."

The power was still out and it was getting dark. "Let's grill up some hamburgers for supper, go to bed early and get a fresh start on this tomorrow." They all agreed.

The power was still off when they went to bed. It was really dark and real quiet. Until midnight. They were quickly and rudely awakened by bright lights and the loud blaring of the TV.

"What in the world...?" The Big Bobber stumbled out of his bedroom, slowly rubbing his eyes.

"Guess I forgot that the lights and TV had been on when the power went out."

"Well, we're back in business now. And you lucked out, Jay. Now that the power is back on, you won't have to use the outhouse."

Monday morning dawned sunny and calm. Mother Nature had gotten over her temper tantrum of the day before and she was now all bright and cheerful.

As they ate breakfast, Jay asked about his friends.

"Jackie and Jody will be coming up for the summer this coming Saturday," C.C. reported. "And Harvey will be around again most of this summer; he should be here next week. And I heard that Leechman's kids will be around for most of the summer."

Clean up work started right after breakfast. They had a chainsaw. The motor was big and as long as the chain bar. It was heavy but it was sharp and could cut wood. C.C. fired it up and The Big Bobber grabbed an axe. "Jay," he said, "we'll do the cutting up and you can start dragging branches out into a pile."

It was a mess. They started cutting up the numerous trees and big branches that were down. At noon, they broke for lunch. "Let's work for a couple more hours after we eat and then let the rest go until tomorrow," C.C. suggested. The other two readily agreed. "Good idea."

When they went back outside, The Big Bobber said, "Jay, how about if you hook the little trailer up behind the tractor and start picking up the wood that we've cut up into handling wood length. It all then needs to be stacked on a couple of new piles."

"The hardwood and the pine need to be in separate piles," C.C. said. "Why?"

"The maple, oak and other hardwood, we'll burn in the house this winter. The pine is what we'll burn in the outside firepit in the summer. We'll have little fires that we can sit around at night. It'll be better than TV."

By late that afternoon, they had many of the downed trees and the big branches cut up. Jay had started two new wood piles with the newly cut-up firewood. The hardwood would have to age for a year or more before they would burn in in the house.

They made good progress, but there was still a lot of wood that needed to be cut, picked up and stacked. There were still a lot of smaller branches, leaves and debris around the yard. "We could use a bigger truck to haul all this stuff away," The Big Bobber said. "Besides, you wouldn't want to get your shiny red fire truck all scratched up, would you?"

"No, I wouldn't," C.C. said. "Let's call it a day and get a fresh start in the morning. I think I'll go fishing." He looked over at Jay. "Want to go?"

"Of course! How about you?" Jay asked the Big Bobber.

"No thanks. I guess I'll just stay around here and take a rest."

"He's gonna go and see Norma," C.C. said to Jay. "Don't let him fool you."

They woke up early the next morning to another nice day and start working in the yard and driveway. The trees that were down in the woods would wait until a later day. By mid-afternoon, they had firewood all cut up and placed into neat stacks. They had raked and cleaned up most of the yard with and had put much of the brush into several large piles. The place was looking fairly presentable again.

"You know, instead of hauling this brush away or burning it, we should drag it all back into the woods for rabbits and other animals to live in," Jay suggested.

"Good idea," C.C. said.

Later the next day morning, Fisherman Andy stopped by to see how they had weathered the storm. "It looks like you got hit real bad." He said. "It looks like hell around here."

The three of them stared at him. "What?"

"Well, yeah. You have piles of brush and stumps and…"

"We've been working on it!" C.C. snapped.

Just then, Abbie drove up the driveway, peeking over the steering wheel of her old Hudson. Harvey and Willie got out of her car. They had just gotten to their grandmother's house yesterday.

Abbie looked around the yard. "Wow! You guys really got hit hard!" She said. "You should start cleaning things up. Here, Harvey can help you get this place ship shape!"

C.C. shook his head. Then he and The Big Bobber and Jay just looked at each other and sat down in the lawn chairs.

16

Jay's Junkyard Birthday

June 22. Jay's 14th birthday. He woke up to the smell of coffee, bacon and French toast. "C'mon, Jay. Get yourself up. The morning's almost over."

Jay squinted at the clock by his bed. 7:30. No, the morning's not almost over; it's barely started, he thought to himself.

"Breakfast's getting cold! Get in here and eat. We have a lot to do today," C.C. hollered from the kitchen.

Jay came out and sat at the table. The Big Bobber and C.C had already eaten and sat with coffee cups in their hand. A cigarette was in C.C.'s mouth.

"What's the rush?" Jay asked.

"Nothing special, we just have a lot to do today."

No happy birthday, no card, no nothing, Jay thought. Maybe they don't know or maybe they just forgot. So what? He wouldn't bring it up if they didn't. He assured himself that he wasn't pouting.

"Yeah," added C.C., "we're on kind of a schedule."

"Why?"

The Big Bobber looked at C.C. "Just because. We have a lot to do today," he repeated. C.C. nodded in agreement.

"Like what?"

"We have to get out to O.C Grady's junkyard and look at some stuff," The Big Bobber finally said. "May take most of the morning, then we'll come home and do some fishing or something."

Yeah, like maybe celebrating my birthday, Jay thought.

By 8:30 they were in the Buick and driving into O.C.'s yard. Going through the gate, Jay was surprised at the large number of old cars and trucks; some whole, some stripped. Some good, some bad. Off to one side, sat a number of vehicles that looked like they may run. He hadn't realized the place was so big. Kinda cool, he thought.

They pulled up to a concrete block building with a sign that said it was the office. Inside, it smelled smoky, like something had been burned. "What's that smell?" Jay asked.

The Big Bobber pointed at a large display case filled with rows and rows of old greeting cards. "O.C. got those cards for free somehow. Sells them for 10 cents each. The cards were in a drug store that had a fire. Cards didn't get actually burned but still smell like smoke, even after all these years."

"Does he ever sell any?"

"Naw, I don't think so. They've been here a long time and there never seem to be any less of them."

A door opened from a back room and a thin, grizzled man in coveralls greeted them. "Mornin', boys."

"And morning to you, O.C. We're looking for a cheap set of wheels. Nothing fancy but it has to run."

"Let's go out and I'll show you what I have in your price range." O.C. led them back out though the door.

"What are we doing?" Jay wondered.

"Well, C.C. and I are looking for a second vehicle. Just a beater to use close to home," The Big Bobber replied.

They walked past rows of vehicles, most of them incomplete. A few were intact. O.C. led them over to an old green Checker. "Still runs ok," he said. "Plenty of room inside, with four doors and a couple of jump seats."

"What do you think, Jay?" C.C. asked.

"Looks like an old man's car. Sorry." Then added. "Looks like a cab."

"It was a cab. In Milwaukee. But she still has some life in her," O.C. stated. He sounded defensive.

They moved on. Next up was a big old flatbed truck. Olson's Feed Mill was written on its doors. "Hey, it's an International like yours, C.C.," Jay said.

"You're right. But this one is quite a bit bigger and a bit older."

"Might be good for hauling wood and such around the place," The

Big Bobber offered. He looked under the truck. "Body's not too rusty but the muffler has a big hole in it."

"Yeah, maybe you're right. What do you want for it, O.C.?"

"A hundred fifty. It's a 1950 with not a lot of miles on it. It runs good but needs a new battery. 6 volt you know."

"Huh," C.C. grunted and kept walking.

They passed several other cars before a black four door Plymouth sat in front of them. "What about this one? The Big Bobber asked.

"1954. Runs good. Tires ok. Gotta few dings and dents and needs some tinkering and cleaning. What you see is what you get, you know."

"How much?"

"Fifty bucks."

"Let's hear it run."

O.C. produced the key and it started right up. "Better not run it too long," he cautioned. "Not much gas in it. But you can take it for a short spin around the yard if you want."

The Big Bobber opened the driver's door and motioned Jay inside. "You drive."

"Me? Drive? I don't know how to drive!"

"Come on, I'll show you." O.C. got into the passenger seat. "First of all, put the clutch in-the pedal on your left. Good. Then put the transmission in first gear. Pull that lever toward you and down. Then let the clutch out and give it a little gas. Real slow."

Jay did as he was told but the car leaped forward with a lurch and took off through the yard. A couple of startled chickens and three dogs dove for cover under other junk cars.

"Too fast! Use the brake to slow down. That's the pedal in the middle. Good. Now just keep steering around things; we can't have you hitting anything."

Jay finally got control and they ended back where they started without any further incident.

"Well, what do ya think, Jay?" C.C. asked.

"Cool."

"We'll take it," said C.C. "Now, what about that old feed mill truck? Throw that in for a hundred fifty for both?"

O.C. thought for a moment. "$175 and I'll tell you what" he said.

"I'll take care of the paperwork right now and you can take the truck with you since you have an extra driver. I'll deliver the Plymouth to you later today-no extra charge."

An agreement was reached and they left soon after, Jay and The Big Bobber in the Buick. C.C roared out of the yard ahead of them in the 'new', noisy, smoking and unlicensed International.

Later that afternoon, O.C. showed up at Hoot Owl Hollow with the old Plymouth on the back of his wrecker. "Here you go, boys," he said, unhooking it.

C.C. and The Big Bobber stood by it with Jay between them. "Happy Birthday, Jay. It's yours." The Big Bobber also gave Jay an old faded birthday card. It smelled like smoke.

"What? You're kidding."

"No, we're giving this to you for your birthday. You're too young to drive it on public roads but you can tinker with it and drive it around the yard.

"My folks will have a fit."

"No, its ok. We'll explain it to your mom and dad and we're sure it will be fine with them."

"Cool," Jay said looking at his new car.

"Now, you can go ahead and park it over behind the shed."

The next day, Jay started 'working' on his Plymouth. His first task was opening the hood. "What the heck?" There was no radiator under the hood.

He went to C.C. and complained. "How am I supposed to drive it with no radiator in it?"

"Well, you ain't driving it out of the yard," he said. "It's for you to tinker on and learn to drive on." C.C. answered. "And only in the yard, on this property. But it still needs a radiator."

The Big Bobber joined them. "No radiator?" he laughed. "That's just like O.C. to pull something like that. We'll get hold of him and straighten it out."

Two days later, O.C. showed up in his wrecker. He hauled a radiator out and set it up against the Plymouth. "Sorry 'bout that, boys," he apologized. "Forgot there wasn't one in it. I got lots of cars to keep track of, you know."

C.C. and The Big Bobber just smiled and exchanged glances. "That's ok, but there's no charge for this now, is there?"

"Naw," O.C. shrugged. "Shoulda been in the car in the first place."

It took him a couple of days, but Jay got the radiator installed. He was proud that he did it all by himself. He also took some parts off the car, cleaned them and was able to get some of them back where they belonged. His great uncles would watch at times, but pretty much left Jay to himself to figure things out. As the summer progressed, the old car was running pretty good. Jay took it around the yard and sometimes into the woods. Scared some squirrels, birds and chipmunks but didn't hit any trees or get stuck. He was still getting used to the clutch and three speed transmission (three on the tree, C.C. called it); once in a while he'd still kill the engine by letting out the clutch too fast but The Big Bobber kept remining him that 'practice makes perfect'"

From time to time, they would go back to O.C.'s junkyard, picking up a few minor parts, but mostly to visit with O.C. and explore his junkyard. O.C. would tell stories about his auto scrapping business; good deals he had gotten; cool cars and trucks that had come and gone. Jay figured there must be money in the junk business as O.C. always had a big roll of bills in on him.

O.C. would let him wander around the yard by himself. Jay liked that. He'd inspect all kinds of old cars, trucks and a few old farm tractors. There were a couple of dogs that patrolled the yard but they had gotten used to Jay and left him alone.

On his second or third visit, Jay met a pony chewing on tall grass between some of the cars. The pony looked at him for a moment, unconcerned, and resumed eating.

Jay asked O.C. about it. "That pony wanders in from the neighbors. There's a hole in the fence somewhere, but I ain't sure where. Surprised my yard dogs haven't gotten out. I don't mind him being there. He keeps some of the grass trimmed around the cars and his owner never seems to care. Thought he might work out as a watch-pony, like a guard dog or something, but he's more scared of people than they are of him."

"He didn't seem to be scared of me," Jay said.

"Well, you ain't particularly scary."

17

Zapping Fish

Jay and C.C. were fishing on Lake Muckawini. It was a calm evening, getting dark. Panfish had been biting ok and they were heading back to their pier. As they neared Hoot Owl Hollow, they saw a truck backing down the road to the boat landing. A new-looking, dark green truck with yellow lettering on the doors was trailering a large flat bottom boat.

"That's a really big jon boat," C.C observed.

Three men got out of the big pickup and stated unloading equipment from the truck into the boat. They prepared to launch the boat into the water.

"That's a State Conservation Department outfit," C.C observed. "Wonder what's they're up to?"

Jay was rowing and continued towards their pier. They tied up the boat and Jay took the stringer of panfish up to the cabin, while C.C stayed on the pier. He was supposed to be unloading the lifejackets and tackle from the boat, but he was watching the newly-arrived lake visitors.

Jay emptied the fish into to the water tank in the shed; they'd clean the fish when C.C. came up from the lake. He went into the house in search of a snack. The Big Bobber was gone. Probably visiting Norma, down the road, Jay figured.

A few minutes later he heard, "Jay! Come on back here! Hurry up!"

Jay ran back down to the pier. The State boat was idling alongside it. A large outboard motor sat on the transom; three high swivel seats sat on the flat deck. A large platform extended part way over the bow with two long poles extending out over the water in front. Large lights were positioned around the boat and several pieces of electrical equipment filled the area between the seats.

C.C. was talking to the men in the boat. He turned to Jay. "These guys are going to shock the fish in the lake. Said we could ride along if we want."

"Shock the fish?" Jay didn't get it.

"Yeah," said one of the state men, who was at the boat's bow. His name was Mark and he was the man in charge. "We use this boat to survey and sample the fish population in many lakes around the state. An electrical current is sent through the water, temporarily stunning the fish. They come to the surface where we can record species numbers and size."

"They said we could ride along," C.C. repeated as he stepped onto the boat. "Want to come?"

"Sure," said Jay. "This sounds cool."

By now, it was dark and the boat's running lights were turned on. As they pulled away from the pier, Mark handed C.C. a piece of paper to read and sign. "This covers both you and us; has to do with permission and liability. We have to use it any time we have civilians accompany us." C.C. quickly looked it over, signed his name and handed the paper back.

The boat headed out into the lake, slowly following the shoreline along the drop off. Powerful spotlights were lit up, illuminating a 6x8 patch of water between two poles extended from the bow of the boat. The boat pulled away from the landing and moved up to the edge of a reed bed. A small generator started up.

"The generator sends an electrical current to the two poles, shocking the fish that swim in the that space area between them," Mark explained.

"Doesn't it kill the fish?" asked Jay.

"No, the current is only strong enough to temporarily stun them. They come up to the surface."

"Then what?'

"Then we survey them. We count them, note the species and size. Sometimes we net them and tag them, but we won't be doing that tonight. We keep moving after we count them; they come to really quick and are soon able to swim off. They're fine. We keep moving, around the whole lake, usually along the drop off."

"What about the fish in deeper water?"

"We can get a pretty good sample at night, just in the shallows. The small fish hang out and the bigger ones come in at dusk and after it gets dark. Besides, the electric current isn't powerful enough to reach any real depth. Wouldn't want a stronger current anyway; that wouldn't be good for the fish."

For the next couple of hours, they continued moving slowly around the lake. Mark stood at the bow, observing the fish in front of him as they came to the surface, yelling size and species information back to another worker who entered the information into a notebook. The third man steered the boat and adjusted their speed, slowing down and speeding up as needed. C.C. and Jay stood out of the way, watching the interesting operation.

Bluegills, crappies, bass, a few northerns and other fish of all sizes, came to the surface between the two poles and the information was entered into the notebook. A few turtles and crayfish also showed up.

Mark called them closer to him to look at a large fish on the bottom. The fish looked sluggish but did not come to the surface. "Looks like a big northern or maybe even a muskie," Mark observed, "but its kind of hard to see."

"This is really neat," Jay said. "Right, C.C.?"

"Yep. I've heard of this being done but never had a chance to see it firsthand. We appreciate you guys letting us come along."

"No problem," Mark replied. "We like to give interested folks a chance to see what we do. Its all good as long as our riders stay out of the way and don't get themselves zapped or fall in the lake."

The operation was completed and the workers started put their gear away. C.C. and Jay were dropped at their pier.

"Thanks. That was really interesting." C.C. climbed out of the boat.

"Cool," Jay added.

"No problem." The state boat pulled away and headed over to the landing.

Back in the house, they cleaned the fish they had caught earlier. They told the Big Bobber about their adventure. He was impressed. "Sorry I missed it."

"We saw a lot of fish and some big ones," Jay said. "Now we have an idea of where and when to fish, even at night."

"Gotta be careful about night fishing," C.C. warned. "It's different than during the day. You know how you get snagged, tangled and backlashed? Well, it's worse at night. Harder to see where you're casting and what's in the water and where."

"I don't mess up like that too much," Jay was insulted.

"Yeah you do, especially when you try the spinning or bait casting rigs. With all the time you spend untangling your lines, I'm surprised you catch as many fish as you do. Stick to the cane pole and you'll always have less trouble."

"We should tell Fisherman Andy and Uncle Tom about this," Jay suggested. "They'll want to know all the new fishing where's and what's."

The Big Bobber and C.C. looked at each other. "Nope," they said in unison.

"Why not?"

"We can tell them about the shocking boat, but we'll just to keep the specific fish details our secret. We don't need to help them with their fishing; let them both keep on trying to figure things out on their own."

"Besides," C.C. added, "You know that neither one of them would tell us if they were in our shoes."

18

Summer School...with pay

Jay stood at the end of the Hoot Owl Hollow driveway. It was 10 minutes to eight on a sunny Monday morning. He carried a lunch box, just like a real worker. He was waiting for the bus to come and take him to his new job. The bus soon came into view. It was actually a school bus but was painted dark green instead of bright yellow. It had Wisconsin Conservation Department written in small, white letters on its side. Jay thought it looked like a prison bus. The bus stopped, the door opened and Jay stepped inside to join 11 other teenage boys on board.

Jay's 14th birthday had been three days ago and he was now old enough to participate in the Conservation Department's Youth Work Experience Program. The program had been in operation for a number of years and provided teenage boys of 14 and up to 18 the opportunity to learn about natural resources and develop nature related skills while working under the supervision of WCD staff on a variety of outdoor projects.

Jay had first heard of the program three months earlier. Last March, he was still in school and living at home in Mendota, when his parent "a talk" with him at the supper table.

"I talked to Uncle Clarence a couple of days ago," his mother said. "He called from Hoot Owl Hollow and told me about a summer program that the Conservation Department has for boys that like to be outdoors."

"What is it?" Jay asked.

"It's a program for teenage boys to work on conservation projects;

working in the woods, on lakes and along rivers. Warden Jim told Clarence about it and thought you might be interested.

"Full time?'

"No. it's three days a week; Monday, Wednesday and Thursdays from 8 until 4. It's about 6 weeks long, from the end of June through mid-August. You can learn a lot, plus they even pay a little money for the actual work the boys do."

"How much?"

"I think it's about $1.25 an hour but I'm not sure."

"I thought I could spend the summer again with C.C. and The Big Bobber."

"You can and you are. The program covers several areas of the state and there's a group out of Wakanda so you could stay with them again and join the group of other boys from that area. Plus, you'd have a chance to meet even more new kids your age up there this summer."

It all sounded good to Jay. "Ok, I'll try it and see how it goes." Besides, he thought, it's three months away and I can always change my mind.

"Good," his mother said. "We're all set. I already signed and sent in all the permission slips and other paperwork. You 're all signed up to start up there in June."

"You already did all that?" Jay frowned at his mother.

His mother smiled at him. "Of course I did, dear."

Jay had arrived back at Hoot Owl Hollow the weekend after school let out. He moved back into his summer bedroom and looked up his friends. Harvey was the only one around but Jay was told that the others would be around in a week or so.

Jay wanted to learn more details about what he was getting into with the work program he would be starting in a week and a half. C.C. and The Big Bobber were able to tell him a few things but on the second day of Jay's return, Warden Jim was asked to stop over and better explain it all to Jay.

"As you know, the program is for teenage boys who are interested in nature and conservation, fishing, hunting, camping; anything outdoors," he explained.

"No girls in the program?" Jay asked.

"Not at that this time, but I wouldn't be surprised if it was opened up to them in the future."

Jay thought of Jackie and Fisherwoman. They'd fit into the program; maybe even help teach it.

"There are twelve of you local boys in the program here this summer. You may all be working together on some projects but you'll usually be split up into two crews of six each. The bus will pick you up at 8am every Monday, Wednesday and Thursday morning until mid-August. You'll be dropped off back at home by 3 in the afternoon. Pack your own lunch. The program will provide you with a hard hat, gloves and a rain poncho. You'll have to wear work boots, which the state does not furnish. You'll get paid every two weeks; $1.25 per hour for 6 hours of work each of the three days you work each week. You get an hour for lunch but don't get paid for it.

Warden Jim took a breath and continued, "You'll learn a lot about animals, birds and fish. You'll spend most of the time outside unless the weather is too bad, then indoor things will be planned, either at the local WCD office or at the state fish hatchery. You'll have a chance to learn a lot of things. You'll help out sometimes at the fish hatchery. You'll also be working on some of the trout streams and lakes, planting trees, building and putting up bluebird houses and wood duck houses, maybe do another ride along or two, help make hiking trails and other things. It'll be a good experience for you. I know you'll like it."

Back to the bus: The bus was pretty quiet even with 12 young boys in it. But after all, it was 8 am on a Monday morning and everyone was probably still half asleep. As Jay boarded, he was greeted by a tall, middle age man with a graying crew cut. He wore green work pants and matching shirt with 'WCD' over the pocket. "Welcome aboard," he said as he checked Jay's name off the clipboard he held. "My name's Slim. I'm your teacher and the foreman for this crew." He checked Jay's name off of a list on his clipboard and handed Jay a plastic yellow hard hat and a pair of work gloves. "Find yourself a seat and get comfortable. We have about a half hour ride."

Jay settled into an aisle seat half way to the back of the bus and sat down as Slim stood up and faced the boys. "Listen up. Today we're going out to the School Forest. There'll be an educational program on the School

Forest and a basic lesson on tree identification as soon as we get there. Then you can eat lunch. After that, you'll be helping plant pine seedlings until we quit and head back about 2:30."

A couple hands went up. "No questions right now, ok? Once we get there you can ask anything you want."

Seated next to Jay was a tall boy with bright red hair, combed back into a duck tail. "Hey, I'm Sparky."

"Hey, I'm Jay.

Sparky turned to the seat behind him. "And behind me is Billy, but we call him Butch 'cuz his dad's the local butcher at the meat market." Butch leaned up. "Hi."

Another kid leaned over from the seat in front of them. "I'm Dudley but call me Dud. I seen you around last summer. On the lake and all."

"Yeah," Jay said.

"And over there is Loon."

"Loon?"

"Yeah, his real name is Eugene but he likes to be called Loon. He's a little nuts but he's ok. Pretty cool, but you never know what he's gonna do or say next."

They soon got off the bus at the School Forest. The morning programs were interesting enough. After lunch, under Slim's supervision, they learned about planting seedlings. Slim pulled a 2-bottom plow behind a tractor, while some of the boys put seedlings in the open row. The other boys followed the slow-moving machine, filling in the rows and packing dirt around the seedlings. The rest of the boys carried boxes of seedlings to the machine. It was hard at first but got easier once they got into a rhythm. To be fair, Slim had them rotate every once in a while so no one was stuck doing the same job all afternoon. When it was time to quit, Jay felt that the day had passed very quickly.

The rest of the week was also interesting. They went back to the school forest to further their learning of tree identification, forest management and even a little information on tapping sugar maples. They continued planting seedlings in the afternoon.

As they rode the bus home on Thursday afternoon, Slim announced that next week, they would be building bluebird houses in the WCD shop on Monday and Wednesday and putting them up on Thursday.

Jay didn't mind being picked up at 8 and he really liked getting home by 3. On workdays, he still had some of the afternoon and the evening to do other things. And having Tuesday and Friday, as well as his weekends free, was nice.

It rained most of the following week but it was ok because they were inside the WCD workshop, building bird houses. All day Monday and Wednesday morning, they built small houses for bluebirds and larger ones for wood ducks. On Wednesday afternoon, the rain had stopped and they went out to various tracts of state-owned land and put the birdhouses up. They spent Thursday putting up the wood duck houses.

They then spent 3 weeks on several area trout streams. They cleared brush and built overhangs out of small logs and brush, where fish could find shelter in the bends of the streams. While working, Jay saw quite a few trout; most of them small but there were a few nice sized ones.

In early August, they worked on a three-mile-long state-owned hiking trail that ran along the Norway River. They mowed and cut brush and spread small pea gravel in certain places. They then had to rake the trail after the gravel was spread. "What a waste of time," Loon complained. "Its gonna get messed up again as soon as the first few people walk on it."

They were kept busy but still had a little time for some fun. During their lunch hour they would play football in their hard hats, using a rolled-up rain poncho for a football. Loon decided to make a chipmunk trap during their week-long trail work project. He dug a steep sided hole about three feet deep and dropped some peanuts in it. "The idea," he said, "is that the chipmunks will jump in the hole for the food and not be able to get out."

"What ya gonna do with them if you catch any?" Boner asked him.

"Make pets out of them and teach them to do things. Like eat out of my hand."

The rest of the group just shook their heads. After checking the hole several times during the week, Loon found no peanuts left in it but no chipmunks either.

"Maybe you should grease the side so they're too slippery for the little critters to climb out," Sparky suggested. He was laughing.

"Good idea," said Loon. But he soon realized that that idea didn't work and gave up on his chipmunk collecting project.

On the Monday of the last week of the program, the bus came to pick Jay up as usual but when he got on, Slim announced, "We have a small brush and grass fire burning in a field about 3 miles away. We're heading over there to help out."

On the way, the boys got a crash course in fire safety and told what their job would be. They would use flat shovels to beat out burning grass. They were warned to keep their eyes open and not get close to any big flames. They were to put out any sparks and embers in the area the fire had already gone through.

They got off the bus and were each issued a shovel and a bandana to wear around their necks. "Keep your hard hats on, wear your gloves and stay out of the smoke as best you can. Keep close to each other. And I'll be right with you," Slim told them. He eyed Loon. "Loon, you stick close to me."

They spread out behind the fire line, beating on sparks. Before long, Slim told Jay, Sparky and Butch to follow him to where a small bulldozer was making a fire lane to contain the fire and protect an unburned part of the field. "Follow a ways behind the dozer-at a safe distance-and swat out any sparks, embers or burning sticks that get cross the lane into the unburned area. Follow the hand signals of the dozer operator. He'll keep an eye out for you guys."

After a couple hours, the small fire was under control and the boys boarded the bus. Slim thanked them for their help. "And today, you get to knock off and go home early. Clean up and have some fun this afternoon. I'll see you Wednesday morning at the regular time."

Once home, Jay told C.C about the fire.

"Yeah, I heard about it already. The news travels fast on the phone party line. An interesting experience for you, huh? Better get cleaned up; you've got a little soot on your face and you smell like smoke."

Jay looked at himself in the mirror and went back outside instead. He rubbed a little soot off his shirt on his face and went outside to sit in one of the lawn chairs. He made himself look worn out when Jackie and Jo stopped by a half an hour later.

"What've you been doing, playing in the dirt?" Jackie asked him.

"No. I helped fight a forest fire."

"A forest fire? I didn't hear anything about a forest fire. And no sirens; nothing."

"Well, technically, I guess it was a brush or grassfire. Several miles up the road; west of here."

"Wow," Jo said. "That must have been scary."

"Naw," Jay replied. "It was dangerous all right but really pretty cool."

C.C. walked past them on his way to the shed and heard Jay. He smiled to himself and shook his head. He kept on going.

Thursday was their last day. They spent most of the day back at the fish hatchery where they had started in June. The Conservation Department provided them with a free lunch and a certificate of completion of the program. They were allowed to keep their hard hats and rain ponchos.

They also got their pay for the work they did in the program. Jay got a check for almost $200. It was his first real paycheck; even had social security taken out. He felt like a grownup.

19

Independence Day

Three of our national annually celebrated holidays are summer holidays: Memorial Day (the unofficial beginning of summer), Independence Day (the mid-summer national birthday party) and Labor Day (the unofficial end of summer). 'The 4th' shares its party title with New Year's Eve, St. Patrick's Day and in some places, Halloween. Most of the other holidays have a more somber tone; honoring someone's birth and/ or death or providing serious recognition to a group or event. Although 'the 4th' recognizes an obviously significant even, it is often a raucous birthday party and is, without a doubt, the noisiest holiday; fireworks, firecrackers, M-80s, cherry bombs and more can be heard and seen across the nation on this day and days preceding and following it.

July 4, 1964 dawned sunny and clear, promising to be a hot day. Lake Muckawini was crowded early and promised to stay crowded all day. The road was busy; a lot of people were around.

C.C. and The Big Bobber had started cleaning up around Hoot Owl Hollow right after breakfast. Jay helped. "We're going to have company later and don't want this place looking like a pig sty," The Big Bobber said as he swept the floor. C.C. was washing breakfast dishes. Jay was drying them.

"I think he's expecting Norma to come over," C. C. said to Jay.

"And I bet you invited Abbie," snapped The Big Bobber.

Jay figured that Harvey, Willie, Jackie and Jody would be over too. And probably Les and Linda, too. No doubt they were by their Dad for the holiday weekend.

Uncle Tom had arrived a couple of days earlier. He had helped C.C. replace the screens on two porch windows earlier that morning and was now resting in a lawn chair, sipping a glass of iced tea. Jay came out of the house with a grape Nehi and joined him. "Don't suppose it pays to fish today."

"Not today. Too many people on the lake. Its too hot and I'm too tired," Uncle Tom answered.

"You only worked for an hour or so," Jay told him.

"Yeah, but a man has to pace himself and that's what I'm doing right now."

There were a lot of festivities planned for the holiday. In Wakanda, there was a parade at noon, followed by a barbequed chicken dinner at South Park. The Mayor and Chief of Police were competing in a go-kart race around the town square at 2 o'clock. Two bands were playing all afternoon and fireworks were planned at dusk at the city beach.

"Can we go into town for the parade?" Jay asked. "There're a lot of cool things going on all day."

"We have too much work to do here before this afternoon."

"How about if I work really hard for a while? Can we go to town then?"

"We'll see."

At about 10:30, Jackie and Jo came over. Harvey showed up a half hour later.

"Where are your grandmothers?" The Big Bobber and C.C both asked.

"She said she'd be over later and the go into town," Jackie said.

"Yeah, mine, too," added Harvey.

At 11:30, Leechman rolled up the driveway in his Studebaker station wagon. *"Leechman's Bait and Tackle: Get Those Fish!"* on the sides. Les and Linda were with him. "Hey," Les yelled. "We're going to town. Want to go with?"

Leechman got out and went over to talk to C.C., who was putting a tablecloth on the picnic table.

"Yeah, I really want to but I have to ask and see if I can," Jay replied. Jackie, Jo and Harvey started to get in the station wagon. They said that they could all go but had to stop by Norma's and Abbie's on the way and let them know. Leechman came back to the car.

"C.C. said okay," he told Jay. "He said they'd be coming into town later this afternoon to pick you guys up and you should meet up with him at 3:30 at the popcorn stand in the park.

"Do you need some money?" C.C. yelled over to Jay.

"No, I've got some. Won't need much."

They were dropped off on Main Street, just as the parade started. There were a lot of floats-some fancy, some tacky; a dozen area high school marching bands; veterans' groups, 4-H clubs, boy scout and girl scout groups, colorful farm tractors and lots and lots of fire trucks. Riders on many of the floats and firetrucks were throwing candy into the crowd on the curb and sidewalk. From a couple of local bar-sponsored floats, unopened cans of beer were tossed to adults in the crowd.

A convertible slowly drove by; it had signs on the door telling everyone to 'Vote to Re-elect Honest Howie Thomas!' A fat man in a white suit and straw hat sat up on the top of the back seat. He waved continuously with smile that looked like it had been painted on his face. A middle-aged woman wearing a fake smile and a lot of makeup and jewelry sat next to him, waving half-heartedly.

"Who's that?"

"I dunno. Some politician."

Several floats went by and then came another convertible. This one carried a pretty, young woman in a red bathing suit and a sash that proclaimed her as 'Miss Wakanda, 1964'.

"There should be a 'Miss Muckawini' or 'Muckawini Queen' or 'Muckawini Princess' or something," Jackie said."

"Yeah," Harvey said to Jay. "We should have fixed up your car as a float and gotten in the parade with Miss Muckawini in it."

"Who'd we get to be our 'Miss'?" Jay asked.

"Helloooo?" Linda butted in. "Me! I'd love to be in the parade."

The gang all laughed. Linda looked at each of them; she didn't laugh.

"And now for something totally different, "Jackie said, pointing behind the convertible.

O.C. Grady was behind the wheel of his biggest wrecker, following the "Miss Wakanda" float. His old truck was decorated in red, white and blue streamers. The wrecker's boom was raised as high as it would go; a flag flew from the top of it. Signs on the truck's doors advertised: 'O.C.

Grady's Auto Graveyard and Wrecker Service: Home of Gracefully Aged and Deceased Cars and Trucks.'

As the wrecker moved down the street, someone yelled, "Hey, that wrecker boom is too high; he's going to hit those power lines!" A nearby policeman on the sidewalk realized the situation and ran out to stop O.C. The parade kept going but the floats behind the wrecker came to a halt as O.C. tried to lower his tall boom. After several unsuccessful tries, he was directed out of the parade line and off on side street. A gap had opened up in the parade line.

Suddenly, an old, rusty pickup truck came off a side street, filling the gap and joined the parade. The truck was loaded down with what looked like a load of trash; he was either heading for the dump or helping somebody move. The driver didn't realize he was in the middle of a parade until it was too late. The rest of the parade moved up behind him and for several blocks, he was trapped. The crowd started cheering and waving at him. The driver must have enjoyed the attention; he waved back and honked his horn until he finally pulled off on another side street and continued along on his original journey.

The Junior High School Marching Band was next playing John Phillips Sousa slightly off key. Following them was a large hay wagon pulled by a team of big work horses. Sitting on bales of hay, a group of young children in straw hats at the crowd.

Behind them came the local animal shelter's float; complete with six teenagers, three dogs and three cats. As it passed by, one of the cats, who obviously was bored with sitting on the float, jumped off and ran into the crowd. One of the girls also jumped down and tried to follow after it, yelling, "Stop, Bessie! Come here! Bessie!" Bessie kept on going.

Then one of the dogs, a huge black Labrador Retriever named Bam, noticed the horses ahead of them and got excited. He started barking and bouncing up and down on the float. "Bam!" yelled one of the boys, "stop that!" Bam didn't want to stop it and kept bounced high and barked louder.

The big horses heard the loud commotion behind them and got spooked. They started moving forward more quickly, not quite running but getting close-too close-to the marching band ahead of them. The driver pulled on the reins but the team didn't respond. He pulled harder with all his strength. By then, the young musicians in the rear rows of the band ahead of the float realized that the horses were heading towards them. They stopped playing, broke ranks and ran toward both sides of the street to get out of the way. By then, a couple of big farm boys ran out of the crowd; they grabbed the bridle of each horse and, between them and the driver, were able to slow the team down and quickly stop them-just in time. The parade started moving again after the band regrouped.

After a couple of minutes, the instruments started up on another marching song and the parade started moving again. Bam was calmed down with handfuls of treats. Bessie, the cat, was still on the run.

After the parade ended, the six of them walked down to the town square. The streets were barricaded with hay bales lined up along the curb all around the square. This was the course for the go-kart race.

Two go-karts sat at the starting line. The Mayor pulled the starter cord and crawled into one that was painted orange and had City of Wakanda painted on it. The Police Chief squeezed into the other; it was painted black and white, with Police written on the side. A young, uniformed officer pulled the starter cord for the Chief. Both racers were large men and barely fit into their machines.

"They look like bears riding tricycles," Harvey commented.

Hardware store owner, Shamus 'Mac' McCabe stood at the starting line. He nodded at the two racers, then dropped a flag, yelling "Ready, set, GO!"

The go-karts roared down the course, loudly whining and buzzing like angry hornets as they went into the turns. On the third turn, the Chief spun out into hay bales and the Mayor took the lead. He stayed ahead of the Chief for the rest of the race; three times around square. 'Mac' waited at the finish line and waved the checkered flag as the Mayor buzzed by him.

The Chief, not to be out done, pulled up behind, got out and walked up to the Mayor's go-kart. He pulled a ticket book from his back pocket and loudly announced, "going pretty fast there, Your Honor. I'm going to have to give you a ticket for speeding." The crowd laughed and clapped.

At South Park, a barbequed chicken dinner sponsored by the Wakanda and Rural Area Fire Department, was going strong in the large park shelter. People were lined up at the wood plank counter that ran along three sides of the open building. Firemen manned the grills as they sweated and turned the seasoned pieces of chicken cooking over the glowing charcoal. In addition to chicken, potato salad, hot dogs and a vile-looking sloppy joe sandwiches could be purchased. Coffee and soda were also listed on the hand-written menu posted on the side of the building.

Nearby, a separate booth, manned by the Wakanda Hunting and Fishing Club, served beer and soda to a large, and growing, crowd, made up mostly of beer seeking men.

The local Girl Scouts Troop sold popcorn and candy. Several church groups had tables of hand-made crafts for sale. The city library had a booth with used books and baked good for sale.

The Wakanda Boy Scout Troop had set up a fake 'fishing pond'. Little kids would get a small fishing pole with a clothes pin tied at the end of the line, toss it over a tall, blue curtain and 'fish'. A scout behind the curtain would clip a small prize on the line and give it a tug. The fisher-kid would then happily reel in his prize.

"That's stupid," Jay said. "Why fake it when there are all kinds of lakes around here with real fish in them. Think how excited those little kids would be to get a real fish!"

"Maybe, maybe not," Jo said. "They seem to be having a lot of this 'fake fun'."

It was getting busy as more people came into the park. Folks of all ages sat on the park benches, at the picnic tables, on lawn chairs they brought with them and on blankets on the ground. All kinds of kids were busy in the playground, on swings, slides and on the big merry-go-round.

A local young, local rock and roll band played Buddy Holly's Peggy Sue on a flatbed semi-trailer 'stage' down the hill. On the other side of the park, an older, county western band in cowboy hats musically told Jimmy Dean's story about Big Bad John.

"Listen to that," Harvey exclaimed, "they're singing about our favorite cop, 'Big John.' Bet he got his nickname from the song."

Someone came up behind Jay and gave him a friendly shove. He turned; it was two of his co-workers, Sparky and Butch. "Hey Jay, what's up?"

"Hey yourself. Just hanging out."

"Us, too."

The city baseball diamond across the road had a bunch of guys playing ball but next to it, the small basketball court (with one basket) was empty.

"There's 8 of us," Harvey said. Let's make two teams and have a game. First team with 20 points wins." Introductions were made and the sides were chosen. They played two games. It was fun. No one got hurt; nobody got angry. But they got a little bored.

They walked down to the beach. It was pretty crowded; little kids, teenagers and adults. Most of the adults were parents with their children. As they walked along the shore, Jay said, "We should have brought swimming suits. It'd feel good to be in the water on a hot day like this. The group all agreed.

Jackie was walking next to Sparky. "I'm a really good swimmer," she told him.

"Oh yeah? How good?"

"Good enough. I'd like to go in; even in my clothes but I'd just get in trouble."

"Yeah? Then why don't you?" he said as he pushed her into the South Park Lake. Jackie stumbled and fell face first in the water.

A whistle blew on shore. "No horseplay!" a young lifeguard shouted.

Sparky was laughing with his back to Jackie when she came up behind him, swung him around and shoved him into the lake. "You want horseplay? Here's horseplay."

More whistles and yelling from the lifeguards. Jay, Harvey and Butch went over to help Jackie and Sparky, who thanked their rescuers by pulling them into the water with them. By then, everyone except Jo, Linda and Willie was soaking wet. They had wisely retreated to a picnic table away from the lake when the horseplay started.

By now, there were 4 lifeguards around them. And the police. An officer, who looked like the one who had started the Chief's go-kart earlier, marched them away from the lake to the building housing the bathrooms and changing rooms. He took their names and informed them that were restricted from the beach for the rest of the summer. All except for Willie, Jo and Linda. "And if there is any more trouble, you will be cited, your parents contacted and you will be restricted from the entire South Park for the rest of the year," he added.

Tired, wet and sullen, the group headed off the beach. Harvey was not too concerned. "Kicked off the beach for the rest of the summer? What a laugh! Summer is pretty much over. And maybe kicked out of South Park for the rest of the year? Most of us won't even be around much from now 'til the end of the year." Although Sparky and Boner lived in Wakanda, they said they didn't care that much either. They soon left the group to go home and change into dry clothes. The others, some wet, some dry, headed to the popcorn stand so Jay could meet up with C.C. at 3:30.

"What happened to you guys?" C.C. as they sloshed over the where he and Abbie were sitting.

"We kinda fell in the lake,' Jay said.

"It was an accident," Harvey added, "but we've been kicked off the beach."

Nobody said anything.

Abbie looked her granddaughters over. "Ok, so Jackie's soaking wet but you're not. Why?" she asked Jo.

"I didn't fall in the lake."

Abbie shook her head and looked over at C.C. He grinned. "Sure, and the others all accidently fell in," he said. "Look, most of you are soaking wet. You need to get into dry clothes. Abbie and I'll run you all home so you change." He chuckled. "But you all have to ride in the back of the pickup."

They changed into dry clothes at their respective houses and met back at Hoot Owl Hollow at 5:00 for a picnic-style supper. They hadn't eaten at the picnic so they were plenty hungry. In addition to the seven kids, the adults included Uncle Tom, Leechman and, of course, Abbie and Norma.

As they were eating, a squad car pulled into the yard. Big John got out. He adjusted his sunglasses and walked over to the picnic table. "Heard there was a little problem at South Park," he said, looking at Jay.

"No sir, we just fell in the lake," Jay said.

"Well, you have to be more careful about that. Could've got hurt or drowned. But you didn't so I guess there was no harm done. Be more careful though."

"Want something to eat, Big John?" The Big Bobber asked. "We have plenty."

"No, gotta get going. Things will be hopping tonight. Just thought I'd check in here and see how everyone is doing. Happy Independence Day." He got in his car and headed down the driveway.

Jay glanced at C.C. who glanced back at him. That was no

'just-stopped-by-visit', Jay realized. Big John had been invited, no doubt to talk to Jay and his friends.

Everyone was still there at 8:30. They had set up a row of lawn chairs by the pier, next to the picnic table they had moved down to the lake shore. By now, thee area was alive with firecrackers and other loud noise makers. Their noise echoed off the lake and seemed to be coming from everywhere. By 9:00, it was dark enough for the Wakanda fireworks to start. South Park and most of the area around it would be packed with people wanting to view the fireworks close up.

"Too many people, too much traffic," The Big Bobber said. "We have good seats right here." And the view was perfect. The fireworks could be clearly seen over the trees along the lake and filled the sky with bright streaks, stars and flashes of color. Their oohs and aahs were drowned out by the bangs and booms. The show was over all too quickly.

They could hear a number of neighborhood dogs barking and howling. "All the lights and noise have sure stirred up those dogs," Jay said.

"'Hopefully, they'll quiet down before too long-once everyone stops lighting off their firecrackers."

"Yeah, I hope so," Abbie said. 'But maybe someone should give those dogs some tranquilizers or something to them calm down."

It was time call it a night.

20

Catfish and Carp

"The stinkier, the better!" Uncle Tom unloaded his catfish bait from the refrigerator. Chicken livers, doughballs and jars of unidentifiable things from some business called 'Uncle Josh's Baits' were put in a large cooler on the floor. "Catfish love this stuff. One whiff and they can't resist it!"

"What died in here?' The Big Bobber asked as he came in and grabbed a beer from the refrigerator. "Oh, It's your carp bait. At least it's out of the refrigerator and soon, hopefully, out of the house."

"It's catfish bait, not carp bait. You know that."

"Carp."

"Don't matter," Uncle Tom replied. "I'm taking Jay fishing for catfish today. Teach him how to catch the big cats. Want to come along?"

"Nope," The Big Bobber replied. "Got things to do. Besides, I don't like catfish much. They're slimy and have whiskers. Don't care for them at all."

"They're great! Both to catch and eat. You could learn to love them."

"Yeah? And what about the carp you catch and keep on dragging home? Don't like carp either; like them less than catfish. Never like them and never will."

"OK, both carp and catfish are bottom feeders so we're bound to catch a carp once in a while. Besides, smoked carp isn't bad. You've had it before, down at the Sportsman's Bar, more than once."

"That was carp? They told me it was salmon!"

Uncle Tom smiled and shook his head. The Big bobber left the room, also shaking his head, but not smiling.

Jay helped Uncle Tom load up his station wagon. As usual, it was full of fishing gear and they had to make room for two metal coolers; the bait was stored in one. Sandwiches for lunch, a couple of Bullfrog beers and a couple of grape Nehis were stowed in the other. Jay, with the backing of C.C. and The Big Bobber, had insisted that the bait and lunch be put in separate coolers.

"Should have made chicken sandwiches," Uncle Tom said. "What we don't eat we could use as extra bait."

An hour later, they arrived at their destination; a county park on White Pine River. Several fishing piers had been erected, as well as picnic tables and a concrete block toilet 'facility.' The building had a door on one side for men and a door on the other for women. Jay used the facilities. He came out and said, "Not bad. That outhouse is cleaner, brighter and less smelly at the one at home. Not a spider in sight."

"And no outside door latches," mumbled Uncle Tom.

They unloaded the car, setting the coolers and fishing gear on a picnic table near the water's edge.

"This is a hot spot!" Uncle Tom told Jay. "The river is deep on this side; right up to the bank. Lots of cats been caught right here."

The bait was brought out. Jay selected a dough ball and mashed on the treble hook at the end of his 20# test line. Uncle Tom put a glob of something that could have been chicken livers on his hook.

"Cast out a ways and let the bait sink to the bottom," he instructed. "Wait a bit and then you can reel it in but do it real slow. Don't rush it."

Jay did as he was told, casting it out towards the middle of the river. He let it sink and slowly started reeling it back in. Uncle Tom had moved about 40 feet down river from him.

After about 5 minutes, Uncle Tom's line went tight; he set the hook. Then whatever he had on the end of his line started moving. "Got one!" he yelled. "Get the net from the picnic table!"

Jay reeled his line in and grabbed the net.

"Good thing I had heavy line on," Uncle Tom said, "or he'd break it off for sure. He's got some weight to him."

As the fish came closer to shore and rose to the surface, Jay scooped it up in the net and retrieved a nice size…CARP.

"Dang it! I was sure it was a cat!"

"You gonna keep it?"

"Naw. Let it go."

Jay eased the fish out of the net and back into the water. The carp swam away, seeming to be none the worse for wear.

30 minutes passed and they hadn't had another bite. "Maybe all the catfish have been fished out," Uncle Tom grumbled.

Suddenly, Jay's line went tight. "I have one on!"

"Set the hook! Don't horse it! Reel it in!"

"I am, I'm not and I am," Jay muttered to himself. "In that order."

Jay worked the fish in towards the shore, where Uncle Tom netted it; an 8-or 9-pound catfish. "We'll keep him!" Jay was excited. "That's the biggest fish I ever caught!"

Jay put the fish on the stringer and set it into the water. "That was fun! I'm going to try for a bigger one!" He mashed another doughball on his line and tossed it back in the river. Uncle Tom didn't say anything.

Before too long, they pulled their lines from the water and ate the lunch they had packed. "Pretty slow going today," Uncle Tom said. "Must not be a good fishing day. Explains why there isn't anyone else fishing. Usually this spot gets pretty busy on a nice day like this."

Jay picked up the trash off the picnic table and tossed it in a big green trash barrel. A swarm of flies flew up at him. In the barrel there were several dead carp, decomposing and stinking.

Uncle Tom came over to look. "Damn!" Uncle Tom seldom swore. "People! What a waste! They should at least put the fish back in the river if they don't want to keep them. Another fisherman may want carp. Plus they're part of nature's food chain."

"What's their part?" Jay asked.

Uncle Tom hesitated. "Not sure," he admitted, "but they're part of nature. Wasteful people! Upsetting the balance of nature!" He finished his ranting and they went back to fishing for a little while longer.

Over the next hour, Uncle Tom caught two more carp (which he released) and a small catfish. Jay caught three more catfish, all a little smaller than his first one. They kept one and released the other two.

"It's time to go," Uncle Tom announced. They started reeling their lines in when Jay's line went tight. "I've got another one!" Then Uncle Tom yelled, "I've got one, too!"

They kept reeling. "Maybe we hooked each other," Uncle Tom said. "Wait, no we didn't. Our lines are not that close together." They both worked their fish. It seemed that their lines were moving together. "This feels funny," Uncle Tom said. "I think we may be hooked to each other."

They saw two fish rise to the surface, very close to each other. "It's two small catfish, on each of our lines but now our lines are tangled. Somehow, they got us snagged together!" They landed both. The fish were too weakened and tangled in their lines that they couldn't release them so the fish were added to the stringer.

They loaded up the car, placed the fish into the cooler and headed for home. Jay was excited about the fish he had caught and was looking forward to eating catfish for the first time. He kept talking about more catfish fishing trips in the future. Uncle Tom was unusually quiet most of the way home.

Back at Hoot Owl Hollow, they cleaned the fish and Jay buried the "innards" in the garden. C.C. had told Jay that all fish guts were to go into the garden; good fertilizer. As they were finishing up, The Big Bobber joined them. "Caught a few, huh?"

"Yeah, Jay exclaimed. "I caught five!"

"Any carp?"

"Not for me, but Uncle Tom caught several."

"That so?" The Big Bobber grinned at Uncle Tom. "Must have used that good carp bait. So, no catfish for you?"

"Um, yeah, I got a couple."

"We kind of caught the last two together," Jay said. "Our lines got tangled but we got the fish in."

"Only two, Uncle Tom? You're always talking about the catfish you catch. What happened today?"

Uncle Tom thought a minute. "Er, well, I wasn't seriously fishing today. I was busy teaching Jay how to do it. Had to do just about everything for that young boy. Didn't have time to do much fishing, myself."

"What?" Jay's voice was raised.

"Hmmm." The Big Bobber rubbed his chin. "Seems like your 'student' did pretty good for himself."

"Yeah, I guess he did ok." Uncle Tom picked up the cleaned fish and headed to the house.

21

Friday the 13ᵗʰ on Lake Muckawini

It was July 13. A Friday. Mid-afternoon. Lake Muckawini was busy; swimmers, boats, canoes. Uncle Tom had brought his new (but used) 14-foot boat up the night before and it was still trailered to his Pontiac station wagon. He was eager to try it out. "Come on out with me," he said to the brothers.

"No way," chorused C.C. and the Big Bobber together. "The lake's too busy. Plus it's too early in the afternoon for any good fishing."

"Nonsense! This is when they'll be biting." He looked over to Jay who was reading the funnies in the week-old newspaper. "Come on Jay, let's go!"

Jay didn't have anything else to do and he liked to fish. Besides, he thought, maybe there'd be some girls swimming in the lake. "OK," he said.

They launched the boat at the public landing without incident. The motor sputtered and coughed and wheezed but finally came to life. "It's been sitting while according to its old owner," Uncle Tom said. They moved out onto the lake; the boat slowly picking up speed. "Its smoking," Jay observed.

"Just warming up."

They made it over to a small cove on the other side of the lake that was known for its abundance of bluegills. They had just caught a few keepers when they heard the loud roar of a powerful outboard motor coming their way. A large odd-looking boat appeared around the bend into the cove, loaded with loud, drinking teenagers and going way too fast. "It's one of them new pontoon boats," Uncle Tom observed. "Going hell-a-sailing with a bunch of drunk, spoiled rich kids, all partying away."

"How do you know they're rich?"

"Someone's parents have to be loaded to be able to afford a boat like that."

The boat, with little freeboard showing, drew too close and crossed Uncle Tom's fishing line. "Hey!" Uncle Tom yelled. The response was laughter and a boy stood up and threw an empty beer can in their direction. The pontoon boat sped off.

"Damn kids," muttered Uncle Tom.

All of a sudden, a dark green jon boat roared out of the reed bed, it's outboard whining in pursuit of the pontoon. "Thank God!" said Uncle Tom. "There is justice in this world! That's Warden Jim!"

Warden Jim quickly pulled up to the stopped party pontoon. The drunk kids were pretty subdued. As Warden Jim talked to them, he pulled a fat ticket book from his uniform pocket and started writing.

Uncle Tom decided to move to a different spot. He waved at Warden Jim as they passed but Warden Jim was too busy with his 'customers' to notice.

Next stop was Big Bass Cove. "I call it that because of all the big bass in here," Uncle Tom announced. "Here, try out this spinner bait of mine."

On his third cast, Jay got a hit and started to work a large mouth bass up to the boat. It was almost there when the knot gave away and the large bass took off, the lure still in his jaw. "Darn!" That was one of my new spinner baits," Uncle Tom bemoaned. "One of my best!"

"Sorry."

This time, Jay put a night crawler on his hook. They caught a few nice size bass, which were released and were getting ready to move to a different spot when Jay made one final cast. A fish immediately grabbed his crawler and Jay set the hook.

"Don't horse him!"

"I'm not."

They could see it was another nice size bass as Jay worked it close to the boat. Uncle Tom grabbed the landing net; he wasn't taking any chances on losing this one. "Good one!" He declared as the fish was steered into the net.

Jay yelled, "Look, there's the lure you lost!" Sure enough, the recently lost spinnerbait was still hooked in the captured fish's jaw. "It's the same fish from before!" They worked both baits out and released the fish to the water.

"After all that, he deserves to be set free," Jay said. Uncle Tom agreed.

Next stop was a reed bed by the Muckawini Creek inlet. "Bluegill Heaven," Uncle Tom announced. "Pieces of night crawlers."

Jay baited up and casted. Two things happened at once: the hook got snagged on life cushion in the boat and the rod and reel slipped out of Jay's hand and sank in the lake.

"What did you do?

"I goofed up."

"Well, maybe we can retrieve it." Uncle Tom unsnagged the hook from the life cushion. "Here, carefully pull the line in. Maybe the whole rig will come up with it. Jay pulled and pulled but rod and reel were not coming up. "I don't get it; it's not over 15 feet deep here."

"I bet the bail is still open on your spinning reel and you're just peeling the line off it. How much line did you have on it?"

"I dunno. Looked like a lot."

"Well, keep on pulling and let's see what happens. Hope your knot holding the line on the spool is tight."

Jay kept pulling line in by hand and finally he felt some resistance and then the rig stated rising to the surface and was brought into the boat. Jay looked at the big pool of line at his feet and sadly said, "I think I'm done fishing for this trip."

"Yeah, we can go in. This trip seems to have been jinxed from the get-go. Wrap up all that line and stuff it in your tacklebox. We'll throw it all in the trash when we get home. Don't want any birds or fish to get tangled up in it."

On the way back to the landing, they heard the sound of another loud boat. This one was an old runabout that was moving fast but was courteous enough to stay away from the other boats on the lake. There were two younger guys in it.

"Pretty loud," Jay said.

"Yeah, it almost sounds like a big V8 car engine with no muffler. That's a pretty small boat for a big motor. The boat suddenly stopped in the middle of the lake; it's engine quiet. It then started up and then took off, only to soon stop again. After a moment, it started up and headed back around the lake.

The hot rod boat was still out there when Uncle Tom eased his boat up to the shore and went to get his car and trailer. He backed it up to the water and told Jay to stand up on the car's narrow back bumper and help guide the boat onto the trailer with the bow line.

Jay did as he was told but when the boat was almost all the way on to the trailer, he slipped and slid off the bumper into the water. Uncle Tom looked surprised, then concerned, then amused. "Are you OK? What happened?"

"Slipped."

"I see that."

Jay was soaking wet. He suddenly heard some soft laughter and turned to see a teenage girl sitting on a nearby rock, with an open book on her lap. "Are you ok?" she asked.

"Oh, yeah. I'm fine," an embarrassed Jay replied.

"The only thing that Jay hurt was his dignity," Uncle Tom added. The girl smiled and went back to her book. Jay's face remined red.

The boat was secured on the trailer and Uncle Tom had just moved his car out of the way, when the hopped-up runabout pulled up to the landing. The girl stood up and walked over to an old GMC farm truck with a boat trailer that was parked nearby. She backed the truck down the landing and the two boys loaded the boat. Jay went over to look at it.

"Neat boat. That's a big car engine," Jay pointed at the large motor in the boat.

"Yeah, we had this 348 Chevy mill sitting around and thought that it'd be neat to put it in a boat. And we had this old boat behind the barn, so...here we are."

"That's pretty cool. I'm Jay. I'm from over there." He pointed towards Hoot Owl Hollow.

"Hey there," the older boy said, "We're brothers, Joe and Don Brady. Live on the farm down the road." He pointed at the girl, "This is here's my girlfriend, Amber." Amber smiled. "She'd rather read on shore than be on water," Joe added.

"You should get home and put on some dry clothes," Amber said, smiling.

Jay blushed again and got into Uncle Tom's car. Uncle Tom just smiled.

Back at Hoot Owl Hollow, Jay and Uncle Tom joined C.C. and the Big Bobber on the porch and told them of their misfortunes. "How'd the boat run, Uncle Tom?" C. C. wanted to know.

"Like a top!"

"It smoked," Jay said.

"So you took a swim in the lake huh, Jay? Got your weekly bath in already?"

"Yeah, but I didn't hurt or break anything,".

"Except his dignity," Uncle Tom put in. "You should have seen him blush when that cute little gal watched him fall in the lake."

Jay told them about Joe, Don, Amber and the runabout. "I know the Brady family. Good folks. Those two brothers are always messing around with cars and stuff. They're pretty good with a wrench. They don't cause much trouble but they sure like their hotrods."

"Guess I'll go find something to make for supper," C.C. announced. "Seeing as we don't have any fresh fish for tonight."

Jay opened his tackle box and started putting new line on his reel. "Well," he said, "After all, today is Friday the 13th. Tomorrow's bound to be better. Maybe we can go out again then?"

22

Birdie and Fanny

A car door slammed. Then another. The Big Bobber set down his coffee cup. "I guess they're here," he announced. C.C. nodded and snubbed out his half-smoked cigarette in his empty cup. The brothers got up from the kitchen table and went out to greet their visitors.

A week ago, C.C. had taken a phone call from their younger sister, Birdie, who had asked if she and her friend, Fanny, could come up and visit them for the weekend. "We want to visit some souvenir shops, go out to eat, play cards and fish some," she said. After a pause, she added, "Oh my. Of course, we want to come up and see you and Robert, too!"

The brothers, probably from a sense of family duty, agreed and C.C. told her they would love to see them. The Big Bobber accused his brother of sarcasm but C.C. denied it.

Birdie's birth name was Bernadette (but no one was ever allowed to call her that) and she was several years younger than her brothers. She was a slight white-haired woman, who despite her age, was full of energy. She talked fast, walked fast, ate fast; she did everything fast.

C.C. would tell others, "She's pretty high strung and has two settings: full speed ahead and stop. She doesn't need coffee to get her going and doesn't use the stop setting much."

Birdie loved to travel; it didn't matter how far or for how long. She loved driving her big Plymouth. And, of course, she drove it fast. Her husband Walter, no spring chicken himself, was retired but still worked their little farm. "Farm?" Birdie would trill. "It's no farm; it's a big vegetable garden!" Walter seldom traveled very far from home. He loved working around their place and grew potatoes, cucumbers, some corn and a lot of tomatoes. He sold some his produce in the summer and fall, but a lot of friends and relatives were regular recipients of bags of potatoes, jars of pickles and canned tomatoes.

Fanny (whose real name was Francesca) was about the same age as Birdie. She was a second cousin to Birdie and her brothers and she and Birdie had been good friends since they had been children. She was a little taller and a little heavier, but more easy-going and less wound up than Birdie...most of the time. Fanny's husband had died years ago. She had never remarried but kept herself busy; usually doing things and going places with Birdie.

Jay wandered up from the lake as the group was exchanging greetings and hugs. "Little Jay!" Aunt Birdie screeched. "Come here! Let's take a look at you! Heard you were staying with these old coots this summer. My, but you have grown. They feeding you well? You look a little thin! Do you have a girlfriend yet?" Birdie flitted from topic to topic like a dizzy hummingbird.

Birdie took a breath and passed him off to Fanny, who immediately hugged him and told him how happy she was to see him. "Its's been so long, Jay. And do you have a girlfriend yet?" she asked.

Jay blushed a little and shook his head.

"Well, let's see what we can do about that!" Fanny declared while Birdie nodded. Fanny's two favorite hobbies were gossiping and matchmaking. Birdie was no slouch at either. Jay wanted nothing to do with it.

Their bags went into the house and were deposited in Jay's bedroom. C.C. had warned him in advance that he would be relocated to the couch on the porch while their guests were visiting. Jay didn't mind. His bed was more comfortable than the couch but at least he could stay on the porch after the adults went to bed and listen to the big AM radio.

The Big Bobber made a fresh batch of coffee on the noisy, old percolator and, full cups in hand, they all went outside to sit on the lawn chairs and 'visit.' Jay followed with a grape Nehi.

After about a half hour of listening to them grilling him about his future plans (I'm only 14, he kept telling them), his school, and his lack of a girlfriend, he had enough. He looked over to C.C. "A couple of boards are loose on the pier. Think I'll take care of them."

C.C. nodded. "Good idea." He sympathized with Jay.

Jay grabbed a hammer and nails from the shed and headed down to the lake. Jay managed to be gone for a half hour before heading back to where the group was still sitting and talking. Jay told C.C. the pier was fixed.

"And here is the working boy," announced Birdie. Jay just smiled. Fanny was telling C.C. and The Big Bobber that they both needed to find a nice woman. "This place definitely needs a woman's touch."

C.C. muttered, "Maybe 'Robert' already has," as he shot The Big Bobber a glance. But neither of them pursued it; they knew it would just give the ladies ammunition to continue their matchmaking efforts.

Jay wasn't eager to sit down and be included in the discussion. However, Birdie saved the day for him by announcing that she and Fanny were going to leave for a little while and do some shopping at the little souvenir shops in the area. She asked if the brothers or Jay wanted to go along.

"No thanks," The Big Bobber quickly said. "We have a lot of things to do here."

"Right," C.C. concurred. Jay nodded in agreement.

As soon as Birdie's Plymouth left the driveway, C.C. turned to Jay. "Let's go fishing." Jay didn't hesitate. They grabbed their gear and headed for the pier and the boat. C.C. eyed the pier. "I didn't know there were loose boards on here." Jay just shrugged.

They fished for a couple of hours and caught enough panfish for a good-sized meal before heading in. They were cleaning the fish when Birdie and Fanny roared back into the driveway.

"What're you doing?"

"Cleaning fish for supper."

"You went fishing? We wanted to go."

"You can go tomorrow."

While supper was cooking, the ladies showed off their purchases. There were a lot of cedar boxes, a lot of items decorated with Indian profiles (complete with head dresses on them) and other things, some tacky, some not. "Here," Fanny announced, handing The Big Bobber a wooden sign that said, *'if you tinkle, when you sprinkle, be a sweetie and wipe the seatie.'* "You must hang it in your new bathroom."

"Uh, thanks," he muttered. C.C. subtly rolled his eyes. Jay laughed.

After supper, the adults played cards. Jay was invited to join them but he declined and went to the porch to read one of his paperback westerns. The conversation from the card game in the other room was tolerable; having to focus on the game subdued Fanny some and even Birdie was a little quieter-but not much.

The next morning, the coffee pot was working overtime and Birdie was listing the things they should do today. "First let's go to town; you guys can show us around. It's Saturday and things should be hopping in Wakanda!"

The Big Bobber and C.C. took C.C.'s pickup. "We have to drive separate; we need to get a new wheelbarrow and need the truck to haul it. This was fine with Birdie, who wanted to drive herself anyway.

"No room in the truck, Jay," said The Big Bobber. "You'll need to ride with them."

Jay frowned but climbed into the Plymouth's big back seat and looked for something to hang on to. After all, Birdie was driving. "What's that?" he asked pointing to a small statue on the dashboard. "St. Christopher, Patron Saint of Travelers," Birdie responded.

"Catholic?"

"I think St. Chris was but I'm not. Fanny wants it up there. She says he'll protect us from my driving." Jay continued to look for something to hang on to.

Their first stop in Wakanda was Schmalz's, the biggest (and only) department store in town. With Jay in tow, the ladies collected several bags of their purchases. Jay obligingly carried what he could for them.

After C.C. and The Big Bobber left McCabe's hardware store with their new wheelbarrow and loaded it in the truck. It was time for lunch so they met at Millie's Café. They had just ordered when Fisherman Andy came in, saw them and sat at the table next them. Hellos and 'how-have-you-beens?' were exchanged.

Birdie and Fanny had met Fisherman Andy a few times in the past and knew he liked to fish.

"Good to see you," Birdie smiled at him. "We're going fishing this afternoon. Want to join us?"

"Be happy to."

"Great!" The Big Bobber and C.C. both responded simultaneously. "You're welcome to come along. We'll all use our boat!"

"Oh, wait." The Big Bobber pretended to just think of something. "Our boat is too small for all of us. Why don't you and the ladies just go?" he suggested.

"Yeah," C.C. added. "Us guys have to move some dirt this afternoon. As much as we'd love to go, we really should be doing a little work around the place."

"That'd be great," beamed Birdie." You know a lot about fishing, don't you, Andrew?"

Fisherman Andy just smiled and nodded.

Later that afternoon, Jay helped them load their fishing equipment in the boat. "Sure you don't want to join us, Jay?" Fanny asked.

"Naw, that's ok. Have fun."

The boat was crowded. Birdie sat in front studying her fishing pole, Fanny in the rear watching the lake and Fisherman Andy at the oars. Fanny bought out a small statuette and set it next to her. 'What's that?" Fisherman Andy asked.

"Why, it's St. Thomas, the Patron Saint of Fishermen, Fanny replied. "He'll help us catch fish!"

"I didn't know you were Catholic."

"I'm not, Andrew, but I think St. Tom was," Fanny replied.

Jay stood by the old boat house and watched Fisherman Andy pulling hard on the oars. The boat wasn't moving. Its back end swung free from the pier but the bow didn't budge.

"Pull harder, Andrew," Fanny suggested. Fisherman Andy did but to no avail. The boat still wouldn't move. Finally Birdie looked up. "Well, we're still tied to the pier," she announced.

"Why didn't you untie us?" Fisherman Andy asked.

"Nobody told me to."

Jay came over and untied the mooring rope for them. The boat swung freely away from the pier. Jay couldn't help but laugh. Birdie twittered and Fanny chuckled. Fisherman Andy just glowered at Jay and pulled hard on the oars, moving the boat out into the lake.

Two and a half hours later, Birdie, Fanny, Fisherman Andy and St. Thomas returned. Fanny was happy, Birdie was giddy, Fisherman Andy was not in a good mood. He carried a basket full of medium size bluegills up into the house.

"How'd it go?" The Big Bobber asked.

"Great," tweeted Birdie. "Great!" Fanny smiled. "Not so great," Fisherman Andy grumbled.

"What happened?"

"Well, first of all, I had to bait their hooks for them."

"I don't like worms," shrugged Birdie.

"Then, half the time, I had to cast for them. They were always getting snagged in branches or had backlashes or something."

"Not true! I casted pretty good," Birdie huffed. "Me too," added Fanny. "and Andrew got his own line snagged on tree branches more than once!"

"Then, whenever they'd catch a fish, I'd have to take it off the hook for them."

"Absolutely not true! Only twice, when a fish had swallowed the hook did I ask you to help me!"

"Say, you guys have some decent bluegills here," The Big Bobber eyed the basket. "Who caught what?"

"Fanny and I caught most of them," Birdie proudly stated. "And without that much help," she added, glancing at Fisherman Andy.

"And how many did you catch, Fisherman Andy?" Jay asked.

"A few," he muttered, studying the floor

"Ah!" The Big Bobber looked at C.C. and grinned. C.C. grinned back.

After an evening card game mini marathon of Euchre and Gin Rummy, Fisherman Andy left and the adults retired to their respective bedrooms: C.C.'s on one side, their guests in the middle room and The Big Bobber's on the other.

Jay stayed on the porch, listening to WLS on the radio and reading a new paperback western. He soon heard some loud rapping coming from the walls separating the bedrooms. Then some giggling.

"Hey! Stop rapping!" C.C. yelled out. "I'm trying to sleep!"

More giggling. More rapping, this time on the wall on the other side

"Dang it!" The Big Bobber shouted. "Cut that out!"

More giggling.

"You old ladies are acting like goofy little girls!"

"You bet we are! We're on vacation and having fun!" Birdie answered with a giggle. "And we're happy!" Fanny added.

"I'm glad you guys are happy, but could you be happy a little quieter? And stop the rapping."

More giggling but the rapping soon stopped and before too long, the snoring began; coming from all three bedrooms. Jay shut off his light, put the pillow over his ears and tried to go to sleep.

The next morning Jay awoke to the smell of coffee and French toast. Birdie had gotten up earlier and had taken over the kitchen. Jay wandered in and she handed him a glass of orange juice. "Your great uncles are sitting outside with their coffee. I kicked them out of the kitchen; no room for them in here and I don't need their supervision in here when I'm working," she told him. "Now you go sit down somewhere too."

Everyone soon sat down to eggs, French toast, coffee, juice and slices of some sort of meat. "What's that? Jay asked.

"Spam."

"What's Spam?"

"It's just like ham."

"Not really," C.C. said. "It's left over pig parts. I should know; we had it a lot during the war. I don't want any."

"It's not that bad tasting," The Big Bobber said.

"It's really good," added Fanny. "Here, try some." She passed the plate to Jay. He tried it. It wasn't bad. Especially if you didn't think about what all might have gone into making it.

They finished eating. C. C left to go to the little store down the road to pick up the Sunday paper. He would pick up a copy of the Milwaukee Journal every Sunday morning. Milwaukee was quite a distance from Wakanda but the Journal was the only state-wide paper stocked locally. The Chicago Tribune was also available on Sunday mornings but C.C. did not like the Trib.

Jay helped dry dishes as Birdie and Fanny cleaned up.

The adults then sat at the table, had more coffee and discussed the news that was in the paper. Jay went outside to fill the bird feeders. When he returned, Birdie and Fanny's suitcases were being loaded into the Plymouth. They were ready to head home. "Don't forget our leftover fish," Birdie yelled to C.C.

Hugs, goodbyes and 'thank-yous' were shared and Birdie roared out of the driveway. Jay watched the dust settle in road. "It was nice to have them here for a little visit."

"Yeah, it was," agreed The Big Bobber. "But sometimes a little goes a long ways."

23

The Light Show

A regular activity at Hoot Owl Hollow was 'looking for deer.' Several evenings a week, Jay would ride along with C.C. and The Big Bobber as they hit the backroads at dusk, looking for deer. Not to hunt; just to look at. The old guys had a route they would follow, about 12 miles in all, that would skirt around fields, forests and an old state fish hatchery. Some deer would always be in the field, often near a wood line they could run into and hide if threatened.

Jay liked these drives. He liked seeing deer, especially when they were with fawns. They would count the number of deer they saw. The numbers were somewhat smaller in the early summer but would increase as fall approached and the deer seemed to herd up more. They often would also see other wildlife: hawks, a few turkeys, some possums, sometimes, a fox or two. Once, they even saw a bald eagle.

One night, they were sitting outside. C.C. was smoking a cigarette, watching for raccoons. The neighbor kids were over, hanging out with Jay: Jackie, Jo, Les, Linda and Harvey. They were all bored.

"Let's go out and shine fish," Harvey suggested.

"I don't really want to. It gets boring," Linda answered.

"Me neither. We just did that last night. We do that all the time."

They had been shining fish for several weeks already. The fish shining had replaced night fishing. Shining fish was usually fun; they would see a lot of things in the water: big fish, little fish, turtles, crayfish, clams. They didn't even take fishing poles; night fishing always seemed to end up with a lot of line snarls, backlashes, snags and tangles, which were made even more frustrating by the lack of good light to work in.

"Hey!" Jay said. "Let's go over to the big field down the road and use the flashlights to look for deer."

"Yeah, we could then maybe play flashlight tag in the woods there," added Jackie. "Unless you boys are afraid of the big dark woods."

"No way we're afraid; it sounds like something to do." Les said, "Let's go."

"I don't know, I heard its not legal to shine deer. Hey, C.C. is it legal for us to look for deer with flashlights?"

"Yeah, that'd be ok. No law against that during the summer, as long as you don't have any guns with you."

They searched and found flashlights for four of them. Jackie ran home and returned with a large powerful spotlight. "Got my light," she announced. "This'll shine a long ways." They headed down the road.

The field lay before them and Jackie shined her powerful light on it. The others' flashlights looked like lightening bugs next to it. Several pairs of bright eyes shone back at them.

"There! Some deer! They're eating." Jackie moved the light around and found some more bright eyes. "There're a bunch more of them. Must be at least twenty."

"Eyes or deer?" Jo asked.

"Deer, dummy. Must be 40 eyes out there; that makes 20 deer." They could barely make out the animals in the light. "Let's try to get closer."

They shut off the light and slowly moved towards where they thought they last saw most of the deer. When they figured they'd gotten close enough, they turned the light back on and...nothing. No deer. "Where'd they go?"

"Must have heard us, smelled us or seen us and when they thought we were getting too close, took off."

"I didn't hear them."

"No kidding. That's because they're deer. They're stealthy," Jo said.

"Ooh, big word, Jo," said Jackie, as she swept the light back across the field. No more eyes shone back at them "We must've scared them all away. Darn!"

"Let's keep the big light off and use the flashlights to play tag in the pines."

They moved towards the stand of 25-foot pines at the edge of the field. "Ok," Jay said. "Spread out and hide. I'll be 'it' and try to find you. Once I hit you with the light, you're it, and Jackie, no fair using the spotlight."

"And what am I supposed to do?"

"Well, you just move around; you'll be neutral. If anyone hits you with their light, they're automatically 'it.'"

"Sounds complicated," said Harvey.

"Not really; you can tag anyone else but not Jackie. Being neutral, she makes it a little more challenging."

Jackie agreed to it but was not too enthused. "I want to be able to zap someone with a flashlight."

"Ok, we'll take turns."

They played for almost an hour and then headed for home. Jackie was happily shining her spotlight in the trees and around the field. They soon heard a car coming down the road and as it neared the edge of the field, Jackie pointed her bright light at it. The car screeched to a stop and a very bright spotlight came on; a light much more powerful than Jackie's. She shut the light off and they all ran into the pine trees. They could hear a person talking; it sounded like some sort of radio.

"Oh no, it's a cop!"

They froze where they stood in the woods. The car backed up; its spotlight sweeping over the field and along the tree time they were hiding in.

"Don't move and keep your head down," Les whispered.

The car moved forward again and someone big stepped out with a powerful flashlight. The word, CONSTABLE, on the door could be made out in the glow of the lights.

"Oh, oh, oh!" Jo whispered, "its Big John!"

"We're goners!"

"Maybe not," Jackie said. "Follow me." She led them back, deeper into the pines, moving along the lake. Without using flashlights and trying to avoid being heard, they moved fairly slowly for half an hour.

"Hey, there's the boat landing." Jay pointed. "Hoot Owl Hollow is really near."

They ran to the yard and quickly sat down in the lawn chairs. They had hidden the flashlights just as C.C. came out of the house and walked over to them. "Hi, kids. Been out here long?"

"Yeah, for a long time."

"Didn't you go look for deer?"

"Couldn't find any good flashlights," Harvey lied. "We've been sitting down by the lake, telling ghost stories until a little bit ago."

"Uh-huh." C.C. eyed them. "Well, you just missed Big John. Said he got a call about somebody shining deer. He didn't want to bother Warden Jim until he checked it out himself. He said that whoever it was shined bright lights at him and he figured it was someone up to no good, maybe poachers. He just left here and headed back down the road just now. Didn't you kids see him?"

"We did see a car a while ago," Jay said, not technically lying.

"Wonder if he found any poachers? You kids see anyone else go by or any strange lights shining anywhere?"

"Nope," they all said, almost in unison. "No strange lights."

"You kids don't have any flashlights out here, do ya?"

"Nope," they said together.

"Then what's that?" C.C. pointed at Jay's pants pocket.

"Well, just this one," Jay admitted, bringing out the small flashlight all of the way out of the pocket of his jeans. "This little, old dim one?" He asked. You can't tell good ghost stories with a lot of light," he added.

C.C. looked at them, innocently sitting there, for a minute or two. He started to say something but he then seemed to change his mind and went back into the house.

24

The "Test Drive"

It was a sunny, hot Tuesday afternoon. Being a weekday, the lake was relatively quiet. The road was quiet. The neighborhood was quiet.

"I'm bored," Linda complained. Jay yawned. He was too, sorta.

Linda, Les and Jay were sitting at the picnic table at Hoot Owl Hollow. C.C. and The Big Bobber had gone to town and weren't expected back until later that afternoon.

"Let's go swimming," Les suggested.

"Too hot."

"Let's play some cards."

"We always play cards. I'm kinda tired of cards right now."

"Let's work on the tree forts."

"Too hot and too much work."

"I know," Les continued, "let's take your car down the road."

"The Plymouth? You're kidding. I'm only supposed to drive it around the yard. I don't have a driver's license, remember? And neither do either of you," Jay argued. "Besides, "the car isn't licensed or insured."

"Come on. We don't have to go that far. It'll be fun."

"Yeah, we could drive around the lake and be back in plenty of time before C.C. and The Big Bobber get back," Linda added. "Besides, no one is around so nobody will even see us."

Jay was surprised. Linda was usually scared to do anything that could get her in trouble, or at least get caught. "You must really be bored," Jay told her.

The car was running ok. Jay had been working on it; mostly taking things off of it. There were spots of red primer on its black body where Jay had been attacking some rust spots and filling holes in with Bondo. It was far from a professional looking job but Jay was sort of proud of the work he had been doing on it. "There're no lights on it, no grill and no back seat. No license plates. If a cop sees us, we'll get pulled over for sure and get the book thrown at us. No, I don't mean us...I really mean me! I'd be the one in trouble."

"I get you removing the headlights and grill; you're working on the rust around them, but what's with the back seat?" Les asked.

"The back floorboards are rusty. I'm working on them, too."

"That'll be ok," Linda said. "It runs and stops, right? We can all sit in the front seat just fine."

Jay liked driving the car around the yard but would like to be able to drive it farther. After briefly thinking about it, he convinced himself that it would be ok and kind of fun to go for a little spin in it, but a very short spin.

"OK, ok!" he said. "You guys win. We'll go half way around the lake to the beach parking lot, turn around and come right back home. That should only take us a half hour or so and we'll be back in plenty of time before C.C. and The Big Bobber get home."

"All right!" Linda and Les yelled in unison.

They climbed in the Plymouth's front seat. Jay started the car but let the clutch out too fast and it stalled. He stated it again and eased it out onto the driveway. They were on their way. They pulled out on the road.

A sign said 30MPH Speed Limit. That was fine with Jay. He felt good. His nervousness lessened a little and was slowly being replaced by the excitement of driving his car somewhere.

They had the road to themselves. No traffic. A few people looked at them as they drove by several of the summer lake cottages but nobody seemed too concerned or overly interested in them. Jay sat up in his seat, trying to look taller and older-at least old enough to have a driver's license. He had a baseball cap pulled down to his eyes. He didn't really expect anyone to recognize him but he wasn't taking any chances.

"This is so great," Les said, his arm out the window trying to look as cool as possible. He had called claim to the "gunner" position-the seat by the passenger side window. Linda sat in the middle, trying to find good music on the AM radio. She stopped turning the knob at what sounded like a Beatles song, barely recognizable through the radio's static.

Jay pulled into the beach parking lot and started to turn around. There was a group of 5 or 6 young boys, maybe 9 or 10 years old, hanging around the beach house. They came over to Jay's car. Jay had stopped and they gathered around.

"What a cool car," one of the boys said.

"Looks like my Grandpa's old car," another said.

"But this one's cooler," the first boy said. "Look. No hubcaps, it has primer on it and a STP sticker on the window."

"Are you customizing it?"

"Gonna make it into a dragster?"

"I'm working on it," Jay answered. He felt pretty cool about the attention that he and his car was getting. Even if they were little kids.

"What color you gonna paint it?"

"You ever race it?"

"No," Jay said, "not yet." He pulled out of the parking lot and onto the road.

"Wow," Linda said, "you sure are the hero of the sandbox crowd."

They continued down the road toward home. Jay stayed at exactly 30 miles per hour. He hoped the speedometer worked.

As he went around a curve, they saw another car coming towards them in the other lane. "Oh, no!" It's a cop!"

"I bet it's Big John," Les said.

The squad car went past them. Sure enough, it was Big John. He looked them over as he drove by. Jay kept his eyes on the rearview mirror and sure enough, he saw the squad car stop, do a U-turn and come up behind them-fast. The red bubble light on its roof came on.

"Oh man, oh man, oh man," Jay kept repeating as he carefully pulled over to the side of the road. His hands were shaking on the steering wheel. His passengers were silent.

Big John came up to Jay's window; towering over the Plymouth. "Well, good afternoon, Jay. Out for a little spin?" He then told Jay to get out of the car. "So what's all this about?" He looked the car over. "I need your driver's license, if you even have one. You do, don't you?"

"Uh, er, no." Jay muttered.

"And just what are you doing driving this unlicensed, incomplete car?"

Jay swallowed. "Well, sir, it's a car I work on at home. I tinker with it, trying to learn mechanical stuff."

"Are you planning to customize it? Make it into a hotrod?"

"No, sir. It's only for learning. I just drive it up and down the driveway in our yard and a little bit in our woods. I just tuned it up today and wanted to see how it ran. We just took it down the road a little ways on a short test drive. We're now on our way home. Honest. Almost there."

"I see that. C.C. and The Big Bobber know you're out driving around?"

Jay gulped. "Uh, no. They went to town."

Big John stood by the car and stared down the road for what seemed to be a long time. "Ok, I'll tell you what, Jay. Your great uncles are good guys and they tell me that you're an ok kid. Right now, you're almost home and no harm's been done. But I have to tell you that if I hadn't seen this car myself, I would never believe it even ran. You're missing a whole bunch of parts that should be on it. Plus your muffler is too loud. That's not a glass pack is it?"

"No sir," Jay replied," just a rusty muffler with some holes in it."

Big John shook his head. "Go right home. Right now. I'll follow you. And keep this car there off of the public roads. I'll let you go-this time. But if I catch you doing this again...". He didn't have to finish the sentence.

Big John wasn't done. "I'm giving you a break but don't be telling anyone about that. If it had been any other cop, he would have been writing you tickets all afternoon. And that goes for you two kids, too!" He glared at Les and Linda, sitting silently in the car. They both nodded like their heads were going to fall off.

Big John wasn't quite done yet. "And another thing. I want you to tell your uncles about this yourself. I could do it and maybe I will, but I want you to be honest and tell them about your little adventure."

"Yes, sir. I sure will."

Jay slowly drove the rest of the way to Hoot Owl Hollow and pulled into the driveway. Big John pulled past them and kept on going on down the road.

"Good. Nobody's home yet," Jay observed. He parked the Plymouth where it had originally been sitting.

An hour later, the three of them were playing card at the picnic table.

They had been talking about the 'test drive' when The Big Bobber's Buick rolled into the driveway.

"Hey kids," C.C called to them. "What've you guys been up to?"

"Not much," Les.

"Yeah," said Linda, playing a card. "It's been boring afternoon."

"You know, you kids should find something exciting to do," The Big Bobber said as he walked past them into the house. Ten minutes later, Jay followed him.

25

Sunken Treasure

One Tuesday, Jay rode with C.C. and The Big Bobber on their weekly trip to town. When they went to the Wishy-Washy Laundromat, he walked over to the Coast to Coast Hardware store. He bought a pair of flippers and a diving mask in the sporting goods department. He was going to use them in Lake Muckawini.

A week earlier, Jay had been with Les and Linda on the lake's public swimming raft. Les opened up a large bag he had brought out with him.

"Look at this," he said as he pulled out four flippers and two diving masks out of the bag. "We bugged our dad until he finally gave in and bought this stuff for us." "He scuba dives once in a while, with air tanks and all that stuff," Linda added.

Jay knew what scuba diving was but he had never swam with flippers and a mask before. Les sat on the raft and pulled on the flippers and put the mask over his eyes and nose. "Watch this," he said, as he jumped in the water. He quickly headed toward the bottom, went under the raft and came up on the other side.

"That was quick," Jay told him as he surfaced.

"Yeah, the flippers help you move pretty fast and the mask lets you see things you may not see while swimming the way we usually do." He jumped back into water and surfaced again a few seconds later with a pair of sunglasses. "These were sitting down on the bottom."

"Cool, but those glasses are pretty wrecked up," Jay said.

"That's not the point. The point is that there is has gotta be a lot of neat stuff in this lake, some wrecked up and some in ok shape, and this diving stuff will help us find some of that stuff on the bottom."

"Yeah, but you can't go too deep for too long can you?"

"No, but in the shallow waters and along the drop off we can swim along on the surface and dive to the bottom when we see something cool."

Soon all three of them were in the water, swimming around the raft in flippers and masks. Jay really liked how his mask let him see what was in the water and on the shallow bottom. Because the water was so clear, he could see down to a depth of over 20 feet.

Over the next few weeks, the three of them swam as much as they could, weather and time permitting. Their 'almost-scuba gear' added a whole level of fun to being in the water. They saw fish (mostly blue gills), turtles (all small), crayfish (in the weeds on the bottom) and, once in a while, small water snakes. But they didn't find too many treasures in their searches.

They grew bolder and started venturing further from the raft; following the shoreline, always along the drop off or in shallower water. They also swam off the Hoot Owl Hollow pier and piers of neighbors who would give them permission.

"If you find any treasure chests," The Big Bobber told them," I get half."

They kept their eyes out for big snapping turtles, human-eating muskies and giant water snakes but saw none.

They saw underwater tree branches and brush piles. These usually held snagged fishing lures. They retrieved many different types of lures, some in good and some in not-so-good condition: spinners, spoons, crankbaits, jigs.

They also found other fishing gear. Jay found a rod, complete with a casting reel, that must have been accidently dropped in the water. It was in fairly good shape. A few days later, Linda found another rod and reel in about 8 feet of water. When they brought it up, it had a huge 'bird's nest' tangle of line at the end of the spinning reel. "I don't think that one accidently fell in," she said. "I bet the owner was upset with the backlash and just threw his pole in."

One day, over about 15 feet of water, they saw the outline of a small, wooden fishing boat on bottom. It looked like it had been down there for a long time.

Later, as they sat on the raft, they talked about the boat. "That was so cool to see that," Linda said.

"Yeah," Jay agreed, "this is fun."

"I bet it'd be more fun if we tried this at night. We should get some strong, water proof flashlights," Les suggested. "Think of all the neat things we would see then!"

Jay and Linda both thought about all those neat things they would see: big muskies and northerns with big teeth, big snapping turtles and who knew what else. They turned to looked at Les. "No way!' they said in unison.

Several days later, Jay was looking for something in the big shed when he found a big magnet. He took it out to C.C. "What's this?" he asked.

"It's a magnet."

"I know that, but what's it for?'

"For picking up metal things."

"I know that, but what do you use it for?"

"Nothing, at least not yet. I got it cheap at an auction several years ago and haven't gotten around to using it yet," C.C answered. "It's a strong one; can lift 250 pounds."

"Can I borrow it?'

"Sure, but what for?"

"Treasure hunting."

The next day, Jay, Les and Linda loaded the magnet, now attached to 50 feet of clothesline, into the boat and headed out onto the lake. "So we drag this along the bottom as we row around. Think of all the neat things we'll pick up with it," Jay told them.

Later that afternoon, they returned to the pier with the results of their underwater search: a half dozen nails, a few loose screws, some small unidentifiable pieces of metal and a metal fishing basket with three small, very dead fish in it. "Not much treasure here," Linda said.

Jay stayed positive. "If we do this enough," he said, "we're bound to bring up some pretty neat things."

"Maybe," Linda answered.

A week later, the magnet caught on something in about 20 feet of water. It felt heavy. "What could this be?" Jay wondered. "I can't pull it up by myself."

Les reached over to help and Linda moved to the other side of the boat to balance it. They pulled hard. Whatever it was, it was heavy but they slowly got it up to the surface. "It's a small outboard motor," Jay exclaimed. They carefully got it into the boat. Les exclaimed, "it's an old 4 or 5 horse Mercury!" He knew about these things. After all, his dad owned a bait shop.

The old Mercury's green paint was covered in lake slime and weeds and it didn't look in very good condition but that didn't matter to them. "We have us a motor! We'll just get it running and get to race it around the lake!"

"I don't think it'll ever run," Linda said.

"Let's have C.C. and The Big Bobber look at it. Maybe they can get it running. If they can't, maybe they know somebody who can."

"I don't think it'll ever run," Linda repeated.

They took it home and showed it to C.C and The Big Bobber. "What a mess." C.C. shook his head. 'I don't think it'll ever run."

"I don't either," agreed Linda. "That's what I told them."

"I don't know," said The Big Bobber, picking it up as the remaining water ran out of it. "I'll put it in the shed. We'll take it apart later and see what we have here."

The next week, Jackie, Jody and Harvey joined them in the lake, complete with their own flippers and masks. Over the next month, they found more things: more lures, a reel without a rod, several sunglasses and a full thermos. They also retrieved a small tackle box, half full of fishing tackle.

One day, five of them (Linda was absent) were swimming in a new spot beyond the raft when Jackie brought her head out of the water and yelled," I see something weird down here!"

The others quickly swam over to her. About twelve feet below the surface they could see what looked like a chest or box that had settled into the muck on the bottom.

"What's that?"

"Looks like a box of some sort."

"Too big for a tackle box."

"It's stuck in the muck a ways, "Jackie told them

"How will we ever get it out?"

"Let's take a closer look," Jackie said. She was the best swimmer in the group. She dove down to the bottom to look things over. She came back up a few seconds later. "I don't know what it is but it's a metal, box-like thing about two feet by three feet and it's sunk over six inches into the muck."

"Could you open it?

"No. It's got a little padlock on it."

"Wow! A treasure chest?"

"I doubt it, but I really don't know what it is or what could be in it. We need to find out!"

They went back and told C.C. about it. Soon, they were all in the two boats, the 12-footer and the 14-footer, over the spot. Jackie, Jay and Les were with The Big Bobber in one and C.C., Jo, Harvey and Linda were with C.C. In the other. They had two lengths of rope, each 30 feet long. "Toss the ropes over the side and I'll go down and tie them around the box," Jackie volunteered.

"Ok, but be careful," The Big Bobber said. Jackie jumped in and hooked up the ropes. The Big Bobber and C.C. each pulled hard on the two lines while the kids helped balance the boats to keep them from tipping over. Jackie stayed in the water, making sure the box didn't slip off the ropes.

"It's not all that heavy," C.C. "Thought it'd be a lot harder to pull up."

"No; I guess it's not full of gold coins."

As it came to the surface, they were able to see it better. "It's a locker," Jay said. "Like the ones in gym class."

It was a locker and it had a padlock on it. It was bulky but not real heavy and they got it into the larger boat without a problem. "Let's get it home and cut that lock off. I can't wait to see what's in it."

"A treasure for sure," Jackie said sarcastically as she climbed back into the boat.

They carried it up to the house and put it on the picnic table. Water leaked out everywhere. The Big Bobber produced a big bolt cutter and snipped the lock open. They all circled around to see what treasure lay within. "Remember, I get half of what's in this treasure chest," The Big Bobber announced. "No," corrected C.C., "You and I'll split half; the kids split the other half."

In anticipation, they slowly opened the small metal locker. They all peered inside and saw…. a filthy gym suit.

"What?"

A pair of beat up sneakers fell out, followed by a khaki pair of a boy's gym shorts, a couple of sleeveless tee shirts (once white but now a dirty yellowish-brown) and a couple of slimy-looking towels.

Disappointment soon turned to laughter. "We'll give up our half," said Jackie.

"Yeah" added Jay, smiling at his great uncles. "You guys can keep all of this treasure."

26

The Hunting Party

"Let's do something different and go hunting!"

"No way, Jay," said Linda. "I'm not shooting any animals."

The gang was sitting around the picnic table. They were listening to Leslie Gore crying at her party between intermittent static on Jackie's transistor radio. All six of them looked, acted and felt bored.

"I don't have a gun," Harvey said.

"Hey, I'm not talking about shooting anything. More like a scavenger hunt."

"Yeah, that would be fun. We could divide into teams. Girls against the boys. Me, Jo and Linda against you three."

Les grinned at Jackie. "But that wouldn't be fair," he said. "You know we boys would win easily."

"Not on your life. We'll kick your butts! "Jo responded.

Jay interrupted what could have been a long argument. "Ok. Two teams. We won't make a specific list of items but let's say that each team has to collect at as many cool and unusual things that they can. Both teams get a big sack to collect their treasures in. We'll make separate search areas for each team. This side of the driveway for the girls; the other for the boys. Plus, we'll can keep going into the woods across the road with the same division: girls to the left and boys to the right."

"We have to set a time limit."

"Right. Let's say one hour. Who has a watch?"

Harvey and Linda both did. "It's 20 minutes to 2."

"Ok, at 2 o'clock, the teams will head into their hunting grounds. Be back at 3 with as many things as we can find."

"Whatever we find?" Les asked.

"Yeah, whatever, but remember it has to be unusual things. The team that has the most really, really weird things wins."

"What's the winning team get?"

They talked it over and decided that the winners could have their pick of whatever items the losing team collected. "Now all we need is a judge."

Just then Uncle Tom came out of the house. "Hey, Uncle Tom! Can you help us out and be our judge?" Jackie yelled.

"Sure thing, Miss Jacqueline," he answered. "Happy to help you kids out; always wanted to be a judge."

They told him about their scavenger hunt. Uncle Tom agreed to be their Judge when they returned at 3pm. The yard would be his court room; the picnic table his bench. "Will you tell us when its exactly 2:00?"

A couple minutes later: "GO!" The teams disappeared into the woods.

The boys' team had easy going at first. The woods wasn't very thick where they started out but as they moved deeper into it, the underbrush got thicker and the trees got closer together. First, they found a couple small bones. Jay put them in their team's bag. They then found a gnarled branch, broke off the ugliest part of it and saved it in the sack.

They soon came to a small creek that ran into Lake Muckawini. "Look!" Harvey pointed. "On that long underwater branch halfway across. There are a couple of fishing lures snagged on it!"

Those would be cool to get. "I'll go get them," Les volunteered.

"Be careful."

"It's all fine. The creek isn't very deep." He took off his sneakers and socks and stared wading across. He was almost to the submerged log when he slipped and fell into the water. With some effort, he managed to stand up. The creek was only 2 or 3 feet deep, but Les had gotten himself totally drenched.

"Hey, make sure you get those lures while you're out there,'" Jay yelled. Les sputtered, grabbed the lures and then waded back to shore and deposited them in his team's sack.

The boys crossed the road with Les sloshing along behind them and headed down a deer trail, back into the woods. The trail soon crossed a wider lane. It was overgrown with brush and didn't look like it had been used for many years. They followed the lane.

"I've never been back this far," Jay said. Harvey and Les said they hadn't either.

Before too long, the lane opened up into a field. Just ahead of them, along the edge of the woods, was a good-sized pile of rusted old trash. "Looks like some farmer's private old dump."

"Yeah, from a long time ago. Bet there's some neat stuff in here." Jay started looking through a pile of old rusty cans.

"What's that?" Harvey asked, pointing to a large rusty machine sitting on old steel wheels.

"Looks like an old hay rake or something."

"That's pretty unusual," Les observed. "May we can take it along."

Jay looked at Les and then looked at the big old machine. He just shook his head and continued sifting through the cans. They were all very rusty but he could make out some lettering on some of them: 'Hamm's,' "Gettleman,' 'Blatz.' "These can go into the sack," Jay said, handing four old 4 cans to Harvey.

They continued to slowly walk along the tree line until Jay stopped and pointed. In the underbrush sat a large oval, gray hive. "Looks like an old wasps' nest."

"That'd be neat," Harvey said. He ran over to grab it. "Wait!" Jay yelled. "Make sure there're no wasps in it!"

Too late. There weren't any wasps, but there were lot of ground bees at home. As Harvey picked up the hive, a large swarm of them came out to welcome him. He stepped back but not before he was stung several times. As more bees came for him, he flung the hive as far as he could into the woods. Luckily most of the bees followed the hive. Only a few stayed behind to take their anger out on Harvey.

He scrambled over to his teammates. Les and Jay looked him over. "Looks like you were stung, maybe six or seven times. You ok?"

Harvey nodded. "They hurt but I'm not allergic to them so I think I'll be ok."

They continued down the tree line. After about 20 minutes, Jay said, "I'm not sure where we are."

"Well, the road is behind us somewhere."

"I'm not sure about that. We've been moving around a lot."

"Let's try to head back the way we came," Les suggested. "We're bound to find the road and get back home-eventually."

They moved on. "I don't think we're going the right way," Jay said.

Meanwhile, the girls' team was filling up their sack. They had barely gotten to the road before they found an arrow sticking out of the ground. "Is that an Indian arrow?" Linda asked.

"No, it's much more modern," Jackie replied. "A bow hunter must have lost it. Its been here awhile, the feathers on it are pretty ragged." In the sack it went.

A little while later, they found an abandoned bird's nest. Into the sack it went. Then they found some antlers that a buck had shed. Into the sack they went. Once across the road, they found a bunch of wild flowers. They wrapped them together with a rubber band that Linda had in her hair. Into the sack they went.

"This is easy," Jo said. "There's so much neat stuff out here."

"Yeah," Jackie agreed. "You just have to keep your eyes open for it." She stopped to pick up several bird feathers and put them in their sack.

They came upon an old fence made of railroad ties with some rusty railroad spikes stuck in them. A few of them were loose so they took two. Into the sack they went.

Linda looked at her watch. "We better head back if we want to be there by 3 for the judging."

They headed back towards the road. As they were cutting across to the Hot Owl Hollow driveway, Jo yelled, "look!" They looked. On the ground, by a tree was a small animal skull, bleached white from the weather. Into the sack it went.

They got back to the yard.

Judge Uncle Tom was already sitting on the bench. It was five minutes to three.

"Where are the boys?" Jackie said, looking down the driveway.

"Good question."

So they waited. At 3:20, the boys' team shuffled up the driveway and sat down at the picnic table. Les was still soaking wet. Harvey had spots on his face and arms. Jay just looked unhappy.

"You're late!" The Judge announced. "I should hold you in contempt of court! Where have you boys been?"

There was no answer until Jay quietly said, "we really don't know."

"You got lost?" Jackie almost shrieked. Then she laughed. "And what happened to you two?" She eyed Harvey and Les.

"I, uh, got stung by some bees."

"And I got caught in a strong river current and got swept under water."

"What? You mean that little creek? There's no strong current in that. Plus, it's only a few feet deep at the max."

There was no answer from the boys' team.

Upon Uncle Tom's court order, both teams emptied their sacks and their treasures were presented for judging. The girls' pile was significantly larger than that of the boys.

Uncle Tom inspected the girls' items. He then assessed what the boys had brought in. He made a ruling. "I have to say; the girls' team beat you guys-but good. Plus none of them got wet, stung or late. Under the rules, the girls have a right to anything you boys brought back. You girls want anything?"

"Heck no," said Linda. "Me neither," Jo added.

"Well, I'll take those old lures," Jackie said.

27

Norwegian Walleyes

Fisherwoman had a nice boat; 15 feet long with a big motor, a steering wheel and three seats. It was large enough for several people to comfortably fish off and be able to move around in. She had invited C.C., The Big Bobber and Jay to go to the Norway River with her to fish for Walleyes this morning. C.C. had begged off, said he had things he had to do around the house.

"He's got a hot date with Abbie," The Big Bobber told them. "Don't let him fool you. Besides, he knows we would bug him about fishing for walleyes with a cane pole."

"Well, whatever the hell works," shrugged Fisherwoman.

They had left real early in the morning in order to be at the boat landing by 6am. Jay asked why they needed to go so early and was told that 'the early bait gets the fish.'

The Norway River was a good-size body of water than ran over 200 miles through the north central part of the state. It was known for its walleye runs in the spring. The fish would head upstream to spawn and then head back down river. Both the up run and the down run were known to provide a lot of nice fish. Walleyes were the headliners but the river also hosted a nice population of crappies and other panfish, as well as white bass, northerns and catfish.

After a 45-minute drive, they arrived at the landing and launched the boat into the river. There were a few other cars in the parking lot but it wasn't very crowded. "Looks good," observed Fisherwoman. "You should see how crowded it gets during the fish runs.'"

"Why is it named the Norway River?" Jay asked.

"I guess because of the Norwegians who settled around here years ago," Fisherwoman answered. "Hey, you're Norwegian, aren't you?" she asked The Big Bobber.

"Yep, ancestors came direct from Norway. I'm second generation. I guess that makes Jay fourth generation."

"Norwegians must eat a lot of fish. Wonder if there are walleyes in Norway?"

"Don't know, but I don't think so. The only Norwegian fish I know of is cod; you know, lutefisk and torsk. Torsk is ok and plain old cod is good but Lutefisk…!" He made a face.

"What's that?" Jay asked.

"Fish, I think cod, soaked in lye."

"Ugh!" Jay also made a face.

"Yeah, I don't like it either."

"Anyway," Fisherwoman said, "the Norway River has Norwegian walleyes. Let's get some of them today."

Fisherwoman had brought her large, middle-aged golden retriever, Sinner, with her. Sinner loved being outdoors and liked to ride in the boat. He was usually well behaved but as they loaded a large open bucket of minnows into the boat, Fisherwoman cautioned them, "Keep him away from the minnows; he likes to stick his head in the bucket and eat those he can catch."

They motored down river. When they had reached Fisherwoman's first targeted fishing spot, she shut the motor off and the boat started to drift with the current.

"Good drift," observed The Big Bobber. They started out using larger jigs with minnows hooked on them. Jay was assigned the job of keeping Sinner out of the minnow bucket. After repeatedly being blocked from the bait, Sinner gave up, sat down and watched the water.

They soon had caught several walleyes and a catfish. "Let's keep the catfish for Uncle Tom," The Big Bobber suggested.

Jigging resulted in several underwater snags; Jay lost one lure (you shouldn't have horsed it, The Big Bobber told him) but the others were able to retrieve their snagged baits. On two occasions, Fisherwoman started the motor and moved up above the snag. Pulling on the line from the other direction successfully got the line unsnagged.

A few more boats had come out on the river. Fisherwoman started the motor and they moved back upstream. "Let's do another drift, using Norway River Rigs with a minnow. The rigs will help keep us from snagging on the bottom."

At the end of two drifts they had caught 6 more walleyes and one crappie. "That brings us to 9 walleyes. Let's see if we can get a couple more and we'll call it a day," Fisherwoman said. "We'll do one more drift and then head over by the landing and briefly try there before we head in."

As she was getting ready to start the boat motor, Jay yelled, "Something's on my line!" His pole was bending under a weight.

"Don't horse it," The Big Bobber told him.

I'm getting tired of hearing that, Jay thought to himself. He slowly reeled his line in. "There's something on it but it's not fighting much. Feels kind heavy."

Fisherwoman got the net ready as Jay continued reeling his line in. As it came closer to the boat, The Big Bobber asked, "what in the world is that?"

Jay reeled it in; they could see it was a big, white cotton cloth. "It's a diaper!"

"A what?"

"A diaper!"

"Oh, for Pete's sake! And it looks like it's well used."

"What do we do with it?" Jay kept the diaper at the end of his line, in the water alongside the boat.

"Well, we are definitely not doing catch and release," said Fisherwoman. "Bring that thing in and we'll put in this old coffee can I use for bailing and we'll toss in on the trash at the landing."

Another drift netted them 3 more medium size walleyes. They had caught a total of twelve walleyes, two more crappies and a one catfish (for Uncle Tom).

"Not bad," commented The Big Bobber. Sinner, on the other hand, had gotten no minnows, thanks to the watchful eye of Jay as he guarded the minnow bucket.

As they headed for the landing, another boat pulled in front of them and got there just before them. An older couple was in it and seemed to be having an animated conversation. "I think they're drunk," The Big Bobber said, as they watched the boat pull up to the pier. The man shut down the motor and got out. He held out his hand to the woman.

"He seems ok," said Fisherwoman, "but I don't know about his wife."

The woman handed her husband a fish basket that looked to be full of walleyes. He grabbed for it but missed and it fell into the water.

"Great! Good job, Carl!" the woman shrieked. "There goes our fish!" She unsteadily climbed onto the pier, almost ending up in the water herself. Carl dropped the line to the boat he was holding and grabbed her hand. She leaned on him and they both watched their boat, now loose, drift away powered by the current. "Help us!"

Luckily, another boat was coming up the river and the two young men in it were able to intercept the runaway and tow it back to the landing. In the meantime, the woman, who was more concerned about the lost basket of fish, was making quite a scene.

As she was carrying on, another older man came over and introduced himself to the hapless couple. "Name's Mort Williams. Used to be the sheriff around here years ago and now live next door. Couldn't help but see that you're having a problem."

"My fish!" the woman moaned.

"Be right back," Mort said. He went to his garage and returned with a big pole with spikes on it, attached to long, thin chains. "I'll get your fish back with this."

"What is that?" Jay asked. Fisherwoman had moved her boat up to the pier for a front row seat to the drama at the landing.

"It's what we used to use to drag the river for bodies. You know, drowned people," Mort said, as he tossed the pole into the water. He quickly snagged the fish basket and brought it up to the pier and the woman. "Here you go," he announced.

The woman grabbed the basket and headed to their car without a word. Carl, looking extremely embarrassed, thanked everyone profusely. "Can I pay anyone for helping?" A crowd had gathered, the ex-sheriff, Fisherwoman and her crew, the young men who had rescued the runaway boat and a number of interested bystanders, both on the shore and on the water.

"Naw, happy to help."

"Thank you, again," a very red-faced Carl repeated. He headed for his car. He got his boat secured on his trailer and took off, with everyone on the pier able to hear the drunk woman lecturing him.

"I feel sorry for that old guy," said the Big Bobber

Fisherwoman pulled her boat up tight up the pier and went to get her truck. They loaded the boat onto the trailer and headed for home.

"Gonna have a good supper of walleye," The Big Bobber said.

They got back to Hoot Owl Hollow and unloaded their gear. Uncle Tom had shown up in their absence was staying for a few days, and of course, was waiting for the night's fish dinner.

As they were cleaning the fish, Jay noticed something wrong. "I thought we caught 12 walleyes, "he said. "I only see nine."

Fisherwoman came over. "You're right, we're missing three. I know we didn't miscount!"

They looked in the boat. Nothing,

"Where could they have gone?" The Big Bobber asked.

Fisherwoman looked around, shaking her head. Her eyes settled on Sinner, who was sitting calmly nearby, happily licking his lips. "Oh, no! I think I know where they went."

"Sinner?" They all looked at the big golden retriever. Sinner just sat, licked his lips and smiled at them.

"He looks happy...and full. Good thing we also have Norwegian crappies and a Norwegian catfish," Jay added. "That should be enough fish for everyone."

"Norwegian Crappies?" C.C. asked.

"Don't ask."

28

Labor Day, 1964: The End of Summer

There were a lot of people around. It was the Labor Day weekend and it was crowded-everywhere. The stores were crowded, the lakes were crowded, the parks were crowded, the restaurants were crowded, the roads were crowded.

As it always was, Labor Day was on Monday. By Tuesday, people would be gone, the local stores and motels would lower their prices to the 'non-season' rates and things would return to normal in Wakanda, on Lake Muckawini and at Hoot Owl Hollow.

"I have no need or desire to go anywhere on the holiday weekends," The Big Bobber said. "Too many crazy people and there're more of them every year." C.C. agreed. They didn't have to go anywhere; people were coming to them. They were hosting a big picnic on Sunday and had gotten all their provisions and supplies well in advance.

This was Jay's last weekend at Hoot Owl Hollow. He would go home Tuesday afternoon and start school on Wednesday. He wasn't looking forward to it; he wished he could stay here all year. He imagined how cool it would be to remain after everyone left and how nice and quiet it would be. But then, he reminded himself, his summer friends would all also be gone. They also had to head back to school and although they would keep in touch with letters, they wouldn't be together again until summer returned next year.

Jay's parents and grandparents all came up on Saturday, to spend two nights before heading back home with Jay. He gave up his bedroom for his grandparents to use. His parents slept on couches on the porch and Jay slept outside in a tent for the two days. He didn't mind. Harvey and Les were sleeping in the tent with him. They had flashlights, magazines and the could roam around after the adults fell asleep. Uncle Tom was around, but he slept at Fisherman Andy's house for the weekend.

A big picnic had been planned at Hoot Owl Hollow. The picnic-goers included the usual local adults and kids. Jay was happy that his neighborhood friends, even young Willie, were around for this last weekend. The men were in charge of the main course, fried fish. Abbie and Norma made potato pancakes. The menu also included hot dogs, salads, beverages, desserts and of course recently caught fish provided by the hosts and the guests alike.

It was a little tense when Jay's parents first showed up. They didn't know about his Plymouth. "I thought you told them," C.C. said to The Big Bobber.

"No. I thought you did." The Big Bobber then whispered to Jay, "we should have hidden it before they came."

"I heard that," Jay's mother said. "That would not have been a good idea!"

After his parents were assured that Jay was not and had not been allowed to drive it off of the property; that they had bought it for him to 'just to tinker with' and, most importantly, that the Plymouth did not have to go home with them, they were ok with it. C.C. told them that he and The Big Bobber would be happy to keep it at Hoot Owl Hollow for Jay. The old car would not be adorning their driveway back in Mendota.

His grandpa, Gary, was happy to spend some time with his brothers. As soon as he arrived, the three of them were discussing cars and trucks. They had the hoods open on The Big Bobber's Buick and Gary's Chevy Belair, comparing engines.

"That's nothing but a six cylinder, The Big Bobber told Gary. "You should have gotten a V8 like I have."

"Too much power; more than I need."

"You should get yourself a truck, Gary. You need a truck." C.C. said.

"I've had a couple of trucks in my day. I don't need one now, not in the city."

Jay's parents were out on the lake, fishing. His dad was on the oars. Jay figured it was more of a boat ride as neither of his parents were that interested in fishing. His grandma, Emma was in the house, sewing a pair of blue jeans of Jay's that needed mending.

Harvey, Willie, Jackie and Jo came up the driveway together. Everyone was trying to be upbeat but it was hard, knowing that this was the unofficial end of summer. They settled in the lawn chairs around the cold fire pit.

"We should go to town and hang out for a little while," Jackie suggested. "Our grandma said we could go."

"Yeah, ours too," Harvey said.

"Let's wait for Les and Linda and see what they want to do," Jay offered. "Maybe their dad would drive us in for a couple hours."

Since his parents were on the lake, Jay asked his grandma if he could go into town for a little while with his friends if they got a ride. He told her they'd be back in time for the picnic. "Don't see why not," Emma told him. "Go ask your grandpa and see if he'll drive you kids in."

Just then, Les and Linda showed up with their dad. Leechman told the kids that if they all were allowed to go, he'd drive them all in. Grandpa Gary came over during the discussion and said that he would be happy to pick them up and drive them back home later. That was fine with everyone. The kids could go and 'hang out' for a couple hours in town as long as they were back in time to eat.

Wakanda was busy. Main street had been blocked off and a small carnival was set up. Tents, rides and games extended for two blocks. People of all ages and dogs of all breeds filled the street. A band was playing in the gazebo on the town square. Its song list ranged from country western to polkas to rockabilly to folk, with a Dean Martin and a Frank Sinatra song or two occasionally thrown in. A dozen middle-aged couples were dancing to an Elvis song.

The local Lions Club had a food stand and sold bratwursts and hamburgers. Soft drinks and coffee were also on the menu. Other organizations sold popcorn, cotton candy and mini donuts. The mini carnival rides, most of them designed for smaller children, were busy; lines of kids impatiently awaited their turns. Picnic tables had been set up on a nearby side street. A half dozen tents housed simple games, also designed to attract young children. The vast majority of the prizes waiting to be awarded consisted of tiny stuffed animals.

They bought soft drinks and sat down at one of the empty picnic tables. "Man," Harvey sighed, "I feel sorta old around all these little kids and all these kiddie rides and games."

"Yeah," Jay agreed. "We're kinda caught in the middle; too young for a lot of things and too old for others."

As they sat watching the crowd, the band launched into their rendition of 'The Beer Barrel Polka.' A crowd of people, most of them elderly, immediately converged on the grass covered dance floor.

Jackie jumped to her feet. "Hey! Let's polka!" She said, grabbing Jay by the arm.

"No way! I don't like to dance plus I don't know how to polka."

"C'mon, don't be a chicken." She dragged him out into the crowd of dancers.

The Beer Barrel Polka ended and Jackie dragged Jay back to the picnic table. "You definitely have two left feet. Polkas are simple; they only have a few steps but you still messed it up."

"I told you I'm not good at dancing."

"I'll say! I give up." The next song was a ballad which meant slow dancing, so Jackie sat down. "Let's go play pinball games in the arcade."

They headed to the tent that had a sign that said it was an 'Arcade'. Inside were several pinball machines and a game where a crane picked up a small stuffed animal out of a pile at the bottom of the machine. A silent jukebox in the back charged a nickel a song. 'Out of order', the sign on it said.

After spending too much time and too much money on the crane machine, the boys were disgusted but the three girls each got a 50-cent stuffed animal.

"I want to work in a carnival when I get older," Les said. "Think how much fun that'd be, traveling around the country, meeting all kinds of people, especially girls. And make a lot of money."

"I don't know, Les. Some of those big carnival guys look shady; dangerous even," Harvey said. "Suppose you got in with the wrong bunch?"

"These guys aren't so bad," Les gestured toward some young men working the rides.

"Yeah, well, this is a local mom and pop operation. I'm talking about the big carnivals; the ones that're at the county fairs."

"Yeah, those guys are a rougher bunch," Jackie said. "If they don't like you, you could get yourself stabbed and really messed up."

"Naw, that wouldn't happen. The carnival life would be cool."

"And a lot of those carnie guys have tattoos. The only people that have tattoos these days are sailors and ex-cons. You know, jailbirds."

"I don't care, I still think it'd be cool," Les said.

"Hey," Jay said, "if you want to see the world and meet girls, join the Navy. And then you could get yourself a tattoo while you're at it."

At five o'clock, Grandpa Gary was waiting for them at the end of Main Street. They all piled into his Chevy and rode back to Hoot Owl Hollow. The kids ate at a separate table from the adults and discussed what they should do after supper. They decided to take a walk down the road but it was getting dark and they were back soon. The Big Bobber and C.C. started a fire in the firepit and everyone sat around it, talking and roasting marshmallows. Leechman, Fisherwoman, Abbie, Norma, Jay's parents, his grandparents, Fisherman Andy and Uncle Tom. The kids were outnumbered.

The adults soon turned the conversation to the 'so what do you plan on doing for the rest of your life?' topic. The question targeted all the kids.

"I don't know," Harvey said, starting it off. "I just want to finish high school and maybe go to college. Then we'll see." The adults were not impressed with Les's goal to be a carnival worker. Linda said she wasn't sure. Jo said she wanted to be a fashion designer and Jackie thought she might like to be a veterinarian. Willie wanted to be a spaceman. Jay said he wasn't sure, but he thought he like to work in conservation.

After a bit, the adults decided it was time to turn in and the party broke up. Abbie, Norma, Fisherwoman, Leechman, Fisherman Andy and Uncle Tom left and the others went into the house. The kids stayed seated around the firepit. All except for Linda, who went home with her father. Les stayed as he was spending the night with Jay and Harvey in the tent.

"What was that all that questioning about?" Jo asked. "We have a lot of time to decide what we want to do when we grow up."

"I know," Jay said, putting another log on the fire. "I guess they want us to have some goals."

"Well, my goal is to get through the next school year and get back here next summer," Harvey said. They all agreed.

They sat around for a while longer, watching as the fire burned down and grew dimmer. They agreed to all meet in the morning to say goodbye.

"Well, it's getting pretty late and we have to get home," Jackie said. She and Jo headed back to Abbie's house.

The boys stayed up a little while longer but there was no interest in going out exploring in the woods or down by the lake. There was little to talk about and they were tired. They went into the tent, arranged their bedding and quickly fell asleep.

The fire soon burned out. The owls had been hooting earlier in the evening but had stopped when The Big Bobber lit the fire.

Now that it was dark, they started hooting again.

29

ᑺack to ᕼoot Owl ᕼollow: 2013

It was 10am on a Monday morning in July. Jay and Harvey were eating breakfast and nursing coffee at the Wakanda Truck Stop.

The truck stop had been in the same location for many years, even before Jay and Harvey had ever met. It had been expanded over the years to include a much larger restaurant, a sizable convenience store, a self-service car wash and a much bigger parking area for semi's. The old two-lane highway that had run past the truck stop forever was now four lanes and called itself an Interstate. A three-story hotel sat across the parking lot. Jay and Harvey had stayed there for the past two nights.

They had returned for an extended weekend visit to Wakanda and Lake Muckawini. After eating, they were going to drive together back to Minneapolis, where Harvey would catch his plane to return home to Arkansas and Jay would continue driving on to his home in Northern Minnesota.

It had been fifty years since they had first met in June of 1963. After the summer of 1964, Jay had never returned to spend entire summer with C.C. and The Big Bobber at Hoot Owl Hollow. In 1965, he had gotten a summer job in a local grocery store and was only able to visit his great uncles sporadically, whenever he could get time off and could get a ride up to visit them. Once he had started high school, he had made new friends (male and female) and discovered that Mendota could be a fun city for teenagers, especially in the summer. During the summer of 1966, he had worked at a gas station and was unable to get many weekends off. Plus, he had gotten his driver's license and a car. He continued to visit Hoot

Owl Hollow a little more for a few years but the visits were often brief and infrequent. Jay currently lived in Northern Minnesota and worked for the State Department of Natural Resources as a Fish Manager. After nearly 30 years at this job, he was due to retire in a couple of years.

Harvey's situation, regarding visiting Lake Muckawini, was similar to Jay's. His parents had moved to Kansas in 1966. Although Harvey and Willie still visited their grandmother a couple times each summer, they spent less and less time on Lake Muckawini over the years. Willie was a computer programmer in St. Louis.

Harvey was a tenured professor of political science at the University of Arkansas. He too was planning on retiring in two years. He and Jay had kept in touch over the years by letters (and more recently e-mails), phone calls and occasional visits. They'd been planning a three day visit back to Wakanda for some time, 'for old time's sake.' It had been many, many years since they had been back there together; the last time had been in the Summer of 1969.

This past Friday afternoon, Harvey had flown from Fayetteville up to Minneapolis. Jay had driven down from Bemidji to meet him at the airport and they had driven east into Wisconsin and on to Wakanda for a nostalgic tour of the area.

On Saturday morning, after a quick breakfast and a lot of coffee, they drove out to Lake Muckawini. First stop was Hoot Owl Hollow. The county road around the lake had been widened and repaved; no narrow shoulders, no pot holes. There already were a lot of bicyclists on the road. There were also a lot of joggers. And walkers; some alone, some in groups, many with dogs leashed to them.

"Much more crowded than before," Harvey observed.

"Yeah," agreed Jay. "Hey, did you ever notice that most of these people are never smiling when they're running or even walking? They seem really serious and intense. I think bicyclists seem to smile more and look happier while they're doing their thing."

"Maybe so, but I never really paid attention," Harvey answered. "But I could get a grant written at the U of A to fund a study of that important issue for us."

"Anyway," Jay continued, "and did you ever notice the large number of walkers, and even some runners, with cell phones pasted to their ears? They sure aren't paying attention to the world around them and appreciating the scenery and nature."

"You are so right."

Hoot Owl Hollow no longer existed. C.C. and The Big Bobber had both passed away many years before. Jay always felt that it was good that they both had died at home without having to set foot in a nursing home. It was how they both would have wanted to go. C.C. died of lung cancer; he had passed away quickly. He and Abbie had remained sweet on each other but had never married. She died a couple of years after he did. The Big Bobber died of a heart attack four years after his brother's passing. He and Norma had gotten married and lived together for a couple of years until they both passed away within a year of each other.

Jay had gone to all of their funerals and felt guilty that he hadn't spent more time with his great uncles over the years.

The 'Hoot Owl Hollow estate' had been sold to a dentist from Chicago, who razed the buildings and built a huge half million-dollar house on the site. He had kept and enlarged the boathouse but the old pier was gone. It had been replaced by a longer, wider dock to which a large pontoon boat and a ski boat were tied. A couple of kayaks and a three jet skis sat nearby. A large, obnoxious, bright orange swimming raft floated off the end of the dock.

Down the road, Jay and Harvey pulled over in front of what had been Fisherman Andy's house. It had been extensively remodeled and looked nothing like it once had. It was now an upscale gift and candle shop. Very exclusive and very expensive and open only in the summer.

They went past Abbie's house. Or rather, what was once Abbie's house. The original house had been torn down and replaced by a large 'lake estate' worth more than Jay could imagine. A spotless Hummer and a shiny Porsche were parked outside the four-car garage next to the elegant house.

I wonder whatever happened to Jackie and Jo?" Harvey asked.

"Jackie and I exchanged a few letters a long time ago but it's been twenty-five years or more since we had any contact. Last I heard, she was living in lower Michigan and was the first female game warden hired in that state. She had told me once that Jo had moved to Taos, New Mexico and was an artist."

Next stop was the site of Norma's house. It too had been torn down and was now replaced by a fancy Italian restaurant. Harvey was quiet; he felt especially bad. He had many good memories of his time spent there as a teenager.

They continued driving around the lake, dodging walkers, bikers and joggers. They stopped at the site of Leechman's bait shop. A large convenience store now stood on the site selling gas, beer and other items at inflated prices. Ironically, it sold a limited amount of bait out of a small refrigerator that stood by the restrooms. The original bait shop had closed down many years ago, when Leechman had retired early from his business. He reportedly moved out west somewhere where he had worked as a fly-fishing guide on the mountain rivers for a number of years.

"He must be dead by now," Jay said. "We never heard any more from or about Les or Linda. Wonder whatever happened to them?"

"No idea." Jay and Harvey had both last seen them in '68 (or '69?) and had not kept in touch since then.

They came to the Lake Muckawini Beach. The sand beach had been expanded and the parking lot had been greatly enlarged. A large sign announced numerous rules that must be followed. A small sign near it said 'Tame fish. Do Not Molest!'

"What the hell is that all about?"

A third sign, the largest of them all announced in bold letters the hours that the beach was open. 8am-9pm! No one allowed on the beach after it closed at 9pm! No Exceptions!

"Yeah right; like that rule is always followed."

A number of swings, slides and other playground equipment had been added. Small colored floats, connected by a rope, encircled the large area of the lake designated for swimming. Swimming outside the rope was forbidden and violators were quickly dealt with. The beach was full of kids and adults of all ages. Three lifeguard platforms rose up from the sand; serious looking, well-muscled young men with binoculars scanned to water and shoreline.

"Man, whatever happened to the nice, little high school lifeguards who would play in the water with the kids? Those musclemen in the towers look like bar bouncers."

"Or prison guards," Harvey added.

Across the parking lot sat a relatively new sports bar. It was sterile and large and had outside seating as well as tables inside. Neon signs flashed: The Beach House! Bands on Weekends! Karaoke Tuesdays! Bikers Welcome! There were a dozen new looking Harley Davidsons in the bar parking lot already and Steppenwolf's 'Born to be Wild' loudly came from the jukebox within.

"Things have sure changed since Fido was a pup," Harvey observed.

"You got that right. Want to stop in?"

"I don't care. It is lunch time, we could grab a sandwich."

They went in and each ordered a hamburger and a beer. No Bullfrog beer around anymore, but they had a lot of micro brews.

"It's funny," Jay said, "up until prohibition came along, every town and cross-roads in Wisconsin had a brewery. A lot of them disappeared but after prohibition was repealed, some started back up and continued even into the '70s until it came down to the giants: Budweiser, Millers, Coors and some others. Now, it's come full circle and every town and crossroads has one or more microbreweries."

The bar was busy and getting busier; filling up with bikers in denim and boots and swimmers who had donned flip flops and thrown covers over their swim suits. Some were eating, most were drinking and all seemed to be having a good time. It was noisy.

"Quite the combination; leather and swimsuits," Harvey observed.

"Yeah, I think the common denominator here is having plenty of money. These bikers are obviously rich professionals, weekend warriors, not true 1%'ers."

"That's probably good. Well, at least everyone seems happy and friendly enough. And the music is pretty good." The Byrds were now on the jukebox, singing about being 8 miles high.

They finished their hamburgers and headed back towards Wakanda.

The 'Edge O' the Wilderness' Supper Club was on the grounds of the (relatively new) Wakanda Country Club. A sign assured them that the "Public is Welcome!" Later that evening, Jay and Harvey went in and had a good, but expensive dinner before calling it a night and heading back to the hotel.

Sunday Morning, they took a drive around the now much bigger city of Wakanda. The population had grown significantly. The 'Welcome to Wakanda: Where Nature Lovers Meet' sign bragged of a population of 28,500 wonderful residents. The large population increase over the years was due to a large computer software manufacturing facility moving into the growing 'Wakanda Business and Industry Park' and two major hospitals (One a large Veterans' Administration facility) making Wakanda their home. In addition, tourism had been very aggressively promoted over the past 50 years and had resulted in a lot more visitors (not only in summer but also in the other three seasons) and consequently, more small and mid-sized businesses that catered to tourists.

They spent the morning in town, trying to remember how it had once been, looking for familiar landmarks and noting all the changes that 50 years had brought. Caroline's Billiards was now an antique store. Millie's café was now a micro-brewery/tap room. The Wakanda Trading Post had been torn down (along with several other neighboring buildings) and replaced by the Mega-Mart, a giant supermarket. McCabe's Hardware Store was now a dentist's office. The Phillips 66 gas station became the home of the Wakanda Chamber of Commerce. Schmalz's Department Store had been subdivided and now housed a candle shop, a Christian book store and a fancy Espresso/Latte shop. Unfamiliar stores and shops seemed to be everywhere. The Wishy-Washy Laundromat, looking the worse for wear but still in business, stood where it always had been.

"Well, that was depressing," Jay said as they drove out if town, back toward Lake Muckawini. They had decided that they would rent a boat for a couple of hours and head out on the water, 'for old time's sake.' They had discussed maybe trying fishing for a little while but decided against it. They would need to buy everything: temporary non-resident licenses, rods, reels, a little tackle and bait. They weren't even sure where to go to buy it. There was a huge Wal-Mart out on Interstate but Jay refused to go into that store so that ended that. They ended up deciding that it would be too much hassle for a short time of fishing.

They found a modern-looking marina (Lake Muckawini Marina) and rented a 14-foot boat with a newer mercury 4 stroke motor and took it out for a 4-hour tour around the lake. It was a hot afternoon and kayaks, paddle boards and other boats seemed to be everywhere. A group of about 8 young women, parked in the middle of the lake on paddleboards, appeared to be doing yoga. Several power boats pulled skiers around in the center of the lake and a few others pulled little kids on big tubes.

Soon, a large green jon boat headed towards them and as it came closer, they saw that the sole occupant had on a grey Wisconsin game warden uniform. Jay stopped the boat and the warden pulled up alongside them.

"Howdy," he smiled at them. He was a big, strong-looking younger man. "You guys doing any fishing?"

"Not today. We just rented this boat for the afternoon and are checking out the lake. We used to spend a lot of time in it and on it when we were growing up. We haven't been back on it for a long time."

"No kidding. How long since you've been back here?"

"A very long time," Jay told him, then added, "I used to stay at Hoot Owl Hollow with my great uncles, C.C. and The Big Bobber, in the summer and Harvey here stayed by his Grandma who had a place not far from there. Back in the '60's.'"

"I'd heard of Hoot Owl Hollow and those guys. As you can see, things have changed a lot around here. My grandfather used to be the warden around here in those days and he had a lot of good stories."

"He was the warden around here back then?" Jay asked. "'Would he have been Warden Jim?"

"Yep, that's what they called him. Warden Jim Morgan. I'm his grandson, Mike Morgan. They call me 'Big Mike.' Followed in his footsteps."

Jay told him about the ride-along with Warden Jim and how he had gotten into the Conservation Department's Summer Program because of him and how Warden Jim was an influence that led to Jay's career with the Minnesota DNR.

"Yeah, he was quite a guy," Big Mike said. "He could be super nice or he could be tough as nails when he needed to be. He retired in the mid '70s and passed away about 15 years ago. He got me interested in conservation, too and here I am. I was in another county for a while but put in for this area a couple years ago and was lucky enough to get it."

They talked for a while longer about changes on and around the lake. Obviously, there was much more water traffic these days. "There are still some canoes around but kayaks and paddleboards are the big thing," Big Mike said. "They're relatively cheap and easy to launch and portage. Sometimes there are too many on the lake but it is what it is. What can you do?"

"I imagine you're kept plenty busy. Is there much trouble with so many people being around?"

"Sometimes. You always have some. Most people are pretty good but you still have some that think they own the lake and the laws and rules aren't for them."

"I see the lake is weedier than it used to be," Harvey said.

"Yeah, unfortunately. Some growth is good cover for the fish but if it gets to be too much it can be real problem. There are several big factory farms around and the chemical runoffs are getting into the lake. It isn't a disaster, yet, but it will become one if it's not controlled."

"The weeds don't look real bad right here," Jay pointed down.

"No, that's because of the Lake Muckawini Property Owners Association, The 'Muckawinis' for short." It was established a number of years ago and it has grown quite large and gotten more active every year. The Association does a lot of good things for the lake. For example, they purchased a weed harvester several years ago and use it regularly to keep the weeds cut down in certain select areas."

"What's the fishing like these days? Jay asked. "We used to catch a lot of fish in this lake."

"It's ok but nothing like it was 50 years ago. Between violators taking more fish than their limit, more traffic, changes in climate and water quality and other factors, the number of good size fish has gone down over the years. However, the good news is that what with all of the non-fishing folks in their paddleboards and kayaks, fishing pressure on this and a lot of other local lakes is generally less than before. If you were to get out here early or late in the year, especially on a weekday, you could still do pretty good." Big Mike turned around and watched an over-crowded pontoon boat speeding across the lake. "Well, I better get back going. Nice talking to you guys."

"Same here. Thanks for the update. Nice meeting you."

They figured they saw all they wanted to see on the lake and headed back to the marina, with time to spare.

At 10:30 the next morning, Jay and Harvey finished the last of their coffee at the Wakanda truck Stop restaurant. They had checked out of the hotel before going for breakfast and the car was already packed.

"Well, we better get going if you're going to get your flight on time."

"Yeah, Harvey agreed. "It's time for us to go."

Printed in the United States
By Bookmasters